Have You Seen Me?

Have You Seen Me?

Laura Denham

CARROLL & GRAF PUBLISHERS
NEW YORK

HAVE YOU SEEN ME?

Carroll & Graf Publishers
An Imprint of Avalon Publishing Group Inc.
161 William St., 16th Floor
New York, NY 10038

Copyright © 2002 by Laura Denham

First Carroll & Graf edition 2002

Interior design by Sue Canavan

Library of Congress Cataloging-in-Publication Data is available.

ISBN: 0-7867-1062-4

Printed in the United States of America
Distributed by Publishers Group West

With thanks to my agent, Noah Lukeman; my diligent editor, Tina Pohlman; and to Michael Argo for his unqualified encouragement and support

Pink

Green

PINK

Jaundiced

The newspaper headline says "Still Missing." She's not still missing, that girl. But she always will be, on that particular page, with its big, black font. They become more useful as they get older, newspapers, handy for wrapping breakables and soaking up spills, always more informative in retrospect, once they're dated and yellowing. It's that large, loud typeface, screaming with importance for one day only, true for a limited time. And when you happen across them, soggy or brittle beneath the cat box, weeks or months or years down the road, you wonder how we could have Gotten It All So Wrong, or how Some Things Never Change, or That Would Never Happen Today, and Thank God That's All Over Now.

"Still Missing." Its moment of truth has expired. The paper is from 1997. Revolution in Zaire. Hong Kong Handover. Princess Diana Car Crash.

I've always gauged the real world by its headlines. If I could reference the front page, the big issue, it convinced me I hadn't lost touch, that I wasn't going to be talking to myself anytime soon, writing long, overwrought letters to radio stations, or standing on the street corner handing out single-spaced, paranoid, uppercase rants typed with a failing typewriter on legal sized paper.

And I've always rated my own world according to calendar months and seasons. Like football teams and sales managers and tennis pros. Like everybody else. When I was just seventeen it was a very good year. Suddenly last summer. Now is the winter of our discontent.

It's not about 1997, though, that headline. It's about 1989.

None of this would have happened were it not for 1989. I'd retract that year, if I could. I would go in with tongs and carefully lift it out. Because that one year divides my life neatly into two halves like a deep, septic gash. If I took out 1989, simply skipped from '88 to '90, perhaps I'd be pushing a squealing toddler on the swings of a North Berkeley playground, answering phones in a cube in Sunnyvale, or taking a meeting at Fitz, Brown, Shalit & Flannery on the twentieth floor of an office building on California Street. Maybe I would have a husband, a mutually exclusive sofa and bed, and a refrigerator filled with leftover pancakes wrapped in foil, and two doors' worth of family-sized orange juice and milk.

• • •

Either I have just left home, or I have just arrived there. I can't really tell yet. Either way, it would not be the first time, and maybe this time I will get it right.

I am unpacking again, taking everything out and putting it back in order. My fist is deep in wads of scrunched-up newspaper, as I retrieve, item by item, the unassuming inventory of a normal life. A frying pan, a toaster, a bat and ball beach game, thrown in according to size and geometrical compatibility instead of by category like the man suggested, at the moving company where I bought the boxes.

At the bottom of the carton, my fingertips touch the warm skin of my old shoulder bag. My city-girl-trendy leather purse. I stick my hand all the way in, buried in paper to my armpit, and pull it up. And as it comes out, upside down, a small rectangle of plastic falls out of the front pocket, back into the box where it hides amid yesterday's news. I reach back in and take it between my finger and thumb, wondering for a moment what it could be. A redundant ID card with an unflattering photo, perhaps. An expired credit card. A used up phone card.

But when I fish it out, I find that it is only plain white with a magnetic strip. Two hundred and seven, it says. Insert and remove. I am about to return it to the front section of my purse when I realize what it is. It's the key to a motel room. And I let it go.

There is nothing else in the purse but a crusty-looking ballpoint pen, a sticky vitamin E gel cap covered in fluff, and an unopened envelope, addressed in my writing. At first I think it says "Dad," and start to open it. But at second glance I see that it says "Dan." I drop that, as well.

A couple of balls of newspaper bounce gently to the floor, fragment sentences announcing things in black and white from their tucks and folds. "EPA Rejects—," "Tonight at 10—," "Toxics threaten—," Half a basketball in a player's arm. A columnist's chin.

And there, out of the corner of my eye, I see it. "Still Missing." And next to "Still Missing," there I am. That hopelessly out-of-date college graduation picture, distorted by the triangular creases and dents of crushed paper, my postadolescent eyes, nose, mouth, and cheeks staring up at me in tiny, gray dots.

There I am on the carpet. Screwed up.

Certain sensibilities have slowly dropped off me like so much dead skin. Of course, we're all trying to find ourselves. It's when you have other people looking for you that you know you're really lost.

I was sixteen in 1989. I had dark brown pads on the toes and heels of my feet that stayed until fall no matter how hard I scrubbed. Sometimes I would pour a toxic mound of blue-and-white powdered tub cleaner onto the abrasive side of our bathroom sponge and try to scrub it away while standing in the shower. I would sit on the red steps of our cottage and use a twig to poke the undissolved granules of bleach from the fissures between my toes. I had chronic athlete's foot from ballet practice in old shoes, and my soles were like wet corn bread for three seasons out of four. I went barefoot all summer to dry it out.

Dad had sticky half-moons of black beneath the tops of his fingernails. During the summer months he spent many hours on his back, lying on the cement in the driveway, beside his Indian motorcycle. It was a beauty, a 1947 classic with a low, triangular bicycle-style seat and bright red mudguards, shaped like firemen's helmets, that covered almost half the wheel. The Indian was Dad's trophy bike, and he spent more time massaging the curves of its frame with chrome cleaner than actually riding it. One wet winter, when the garage roof began to leak, he actually removed the gas tank, heaved the bike up the porch steps, and wheeled it into his bedroom, where it stayed, parked on newspaper and shrouded in a greasy tarp until spring.

To get around, he had a Triumph Bonneville, a heavy, oily hunk of bike with the deep, rich engine sound of a small tractor. I preferred riding on the back of the Triumph because there was room for a passenger on the seat itself. With the Indian you were perched up on a grill rack on the back wheel, low to the ground, as though taking an outmoded thrill ride at the boardwalk. I never held on around his waist. Instead I would put my hands on my knees, or loosely clutch the seat behind me.

Dad would say, "It's best to pretend you're a sack of potatoes."

On Sunday afternoons, we would roar around the Santa Cruz mountains until my curly blond hair was tangled thick as a doormat and my eyes ran with tears.

My parents were yogurt-making hippies who insisted I address them by their first names, in that predictable counter-cultural effort to eschew as much as possible of the middle-class family convention. I've stopped now. I don't have to do it anymore.

Dad met my mother, Abigail, at a party in London in 1967. He had been traipsing around Northern Europe making poorly executed sketches of ecclesiastical buildings, contemplating his unlaundered side after years of doctorate-level physics. My mom was a recent Oxford graduate, enjoying an extended picnic on a series of basement floors before settling into a teaching career and a bed with springs and an underneath.

Both of them had attended a reading by Anne Sexton at the International Poetry Festival on the same afternoon. Dad later confessed to having gone there on the advice of a fellow traveler—a young musician from Manitoba who'd told him that it was the best place in the whole of Europe to pick up girls. After a bottle of Mateus rose, Dad faked a convincing interest in "All My Pretty Ones" and nailed my mother to a Fulham carpet for long enough to get her number before the hangover trudged on in.

My mother loved California and the politically spirited surfing community in Santa Cruz. She attained a post teaching English literature at the recently constructed campus of the University of California, and she and my dad settled into a colorful approximation of domestic responsibility.

I know what she looked like only in grades of monochrome. Tall, lean, dark hair, light eyes. The few pictures I have are all in black and white, and there aren't very many of those. My parents left the camera in the woods on a camping trip to Yosemite in the early seventies and never bothered to get a new one. I don't miss her, because I'm not sure what to miss. It was a different story for my father. He held her in his head, I could tell, and he was plagued by the reproductive efficiency of his own memory. He rarely took pictures of anything, afraid that if he tried too hard to capture something it would only be taken away.

"People are obsessed with record keeping," he would rant. "It's an attempt to contain energy, to hoard life's essence incrementally, instead of enjoying real moments, then letting them pass through our lives. If something is beautiful enough at the actual time it's around you, you don't need to recreate it. You remember it forever."

Or so he said. Maybe he was just too lazy or cheap.

Apparently, she looked like Patty Hearst, my mother, and in early 1975, she and my father were almost arrested in a Bay Area record store, until she spoke, and her British accent got her off the hook. I also have a memory, or a memory of a memory, of coming out of a bakery with her, while a long-haired man in a brightly colored woolly hat laughed and yelled after us.

"Hey, Tania," he shouted. "Death to the fascist insect that preys upon the life of the people!"

I knew that there was always a chance I would capture a moving glimpse of her eventually. My mother was visible in the background of a 1966 newsreel film of the Beatles. Supposedly there was a shot of her running along beside their car blowing kisses at Ringo Starr as they pulled away down a mobbed London street. Over time, the image had been used in a couple of documentaries, although I had yet to see it myself. Ringo, of all the Beatles!

I was only four when she died. Nothing quasi-romantic, like an avalanche up at Tahoe or death by drowning while surfing on acid. One day, her heart just stopped beating, and nobody really knows why. A heart attack. It just happens to some people that way.

Oddly enough, while many sixties-era hippies eventually bought cars, warmed up to the occasional TV sitcom, or at least cut their hair if they were not already bald, Dad remained embarrassingly radical for the duration of the 1970s, '80s, and '90s. He kept his glorious, shoulder-length curls and beard, as well as his anticonsumerist ideologies, well past the traditional expiration date. Aside from engaging in the brotherly and vaguely pretentious practice of calling my own father "Tom," I was raised in a household without a car or a television.

Dad's rejection of material trappings was entirely at odds with his income. As an early entrant in the then-fledgling technology arena, he held a lucrative position as a project coordinator at National Semiconductor in Silicon Valley. Just as contrarily, he refused to have a personal computer in the house. Work was the right hand, home the left hand, and never did they meet to shake.

And then there was Dan. Dan McKenna was a kindred spirit of my father's from the job, and his visits to the house a couple of Fridays a month were the closest Dad ever came to bringing his work home with him.

Our place on Lighthouse Avenue was a one-story cottage, its soft, pastel primrose exterior hiding dark wood floors and shadowy, cluttered rooms within. Dan would roar into the driveway on his BSA—his passion for British bikes was one of the many idiosyncrasies he shared with my old man—and the two would embrace on the porch with a manly hug.

That summer in 1989 was the first year I'd been staying

up late enough to consort with them. Since it's impossible now to disallow the entire year of 1989, I guess my second choice would be to turn back the clock and just have stayed in my room.

Dad rolled up his sleeve and slid a collection of socket wrenches and dirty forks to one end of the kitchen table. I lay facedown on the couch in a pair of cutoffs, reading the autobiography of ballerina coke addict Gelsey Kirkland, toes digging into the space between the sofa arm and cushion, feeling for coins and catching matchsticks and other debris between my toes. The light from the fridge glided across my page, then vanished as beer bottles clinked in the kitchen. I glanced up through the adjoining doorway to see the two of them hunched over blocks of perforated green and white striped "computer paper," circling numbers at random, mapping theories, arguing in a language I didn't understand. Dad pounded fiercely at the keys of a calculator as Dan slapped his way through chunks of the heavy bound reports, cutting them with his palm and flopping them open onto the table with a thud and a shudder of glass and silverware quaking under the impact.

"You're so far off, Tommy, you are *so* far off the mark," Dan said, with a woeful shake of the head, stroking his stubble, tucking his long, stringy hair behind his ears.

Dan was about five years younger than my father, and in some unconscious manifestation of flattery or innate need for approval, he emulated him. Both in appearance, and in this ritual, competitive tech talk, which would later degenerate into beer-fed motorcycle trivia and rock history one-upmanship.

"You're wrong, Dan. You can't determine that there's a problem here without looking at the data from April."

"Show me April," said Dan. "You'll see it has no bearing."

"We don't have April," Dad said, sipping beer. "I left it at work."

"Fifty bucks says April is irrelevant."

"A hundred and fifty dollars say it isn't," Dad said.

And so it went on, back and forth, until finally Dad strode into the living room, scooped up his helmet from the coffee table, and rode all the way back to the office.

I had no idea what they were talking about. But maybe, if he'd brought April home to begin with, none of this would have happened.

Dan pretended to do sums in the kitchen, and I pretended to read about the American Ballet Theater. The silence was so excruciating that eventually I went to sit on the porch steps.

Dan's motorcycle was immaculate. I half wondered if he cleaned and polished it especially on Fridays before he came over. There it was, as usual, with its squeaky black tank, electric red BSA badge, and impossibly spotless tires, standing on the grass beside the grimy, worn-out Triumph.

"She's been having some engine problems." The porch creaked behind me, as Dan squatted on the step next to me and wrapped his arms around his knees.

"Nice looking, though," I said.

"Do you ride?" he asked.

"Yes, but I don't have a license."

"Ah . . . Don't do that," said Dan.

It was impossible to go back to my reading with him sitting there, so I closed the book and put it down beside me.

"What are you reading?" he asked.

"Nothing," I said, "It's a ballet book. Well, more about drugs, really. Cocaine."

"That's a big hobby of yours, isn't it?"

I assumed he meant dancing. But I was surprised that he knew, that my name had ever come up in or out of the context of those endless, late-night twists of adult male shoptalk.

Then he said, "I can tell from your body. You're very thin."

Dan stood up, walked over to the BSA, and fiddled with something on the engine. It was just a move, a bit of uncomfortable posturing. I knew there was nothing you could adjust without tools.

"If you're interested, I'll take you for a ride tomorrow."

And he walked back inside, teeth clenched so that the veins on his neck were showing, his skin flushed to the edge of his T-shirt. His pencil had slipped out of the back pocket of his jeans. I picked it up, noticing that it was savagely bitten, not just at the eraser end, but all along its length. The point had been sharpened in an irregular fashion, not with the smooth precision of a pencil sharpener, but hacked away in chunks with a pocket knife. My dad's pencils all looked like that, too.

And it really all started there. I said yes to something I should have said no to. Like the time Dad caught me at age six, pushing a fork into the wall socket just to see what would happen. Everyone was shocked except me.

I kept my hands behind me, even at sixty-five miles an hour. Wind, warmth, and half an hour of the back of Dan's neck. His label was out. 100% cotton, Made in Turkey, Wash with Like Colors. His hair straggled from beneath his helmet, brushing my nose in the breeze. I looked for gray and found a pale, dead strand or two.

On Highway Nine, as we entered Boulder Creek, he made a right and rolled slowly into a residential street surrounded on both sides by redwoods, then left onto a tree-lined dirt road, a dead end. We came to a stop and Dan killed the engine and pulled off his helmet, shaking his hair madly, like a dog getting hosed off on a hot day.

"What's this?" I asked.

"I live here," he said. "Follow me."

We dismounted and Dan heaved the bike up onto its stand. In front of us, the lane narrowed into an earthy path, its slight gradient cut with concrete steps. There at the top, set back about fifty feet from the driveway in a quiet pocket of forest, was Dan's house. The outer structure appeared to be built solely of wood, with large diamond-shaped windows all around its perimeter. It was a geodesic dome. An igloo, cabin, science center hybrid—rustic and space-age all at once.

"I built it myself," Dan said proudly, pushing open the front door.

The place was pretty Spartan, bare except for a large Persian rug, some books, and a couple of pieces of wooden furniture. But next to the fireplace there stood a life-sized metalwork human built entirely of motorcycle parts. I walked directly over to it, gently lifting one of its floppy chain limbs, staring at its gas tank torso, touching its leather pelvis, a re-purposed seat.

"He's part Honda, part Harley," said Dan.

"A Japanese American," I said, fingering the spokes of its hand. In the shiny twin gas caps of its eyes I saw two of myself.

"Sit down for a minute," he said. "I want to adjust the wheel alignment on the bike, and then we'll go."

Dan walked over to the kitchen and pulled a toolbox from the cupboard beneath the sink with one hand, reaching nonchalantly for an open bottle of wine with the other. He tugged the cork out with his teeth.

"Help yourself," he said, "It's an '86 Cab."

I wondered then if Dan knew how old I was. Or how young. Eighty-six Cab sounded to me like a ride to the airport. But I kneeled on his rug with a healthy glass of it, guzzling it like Kool-Aid before pouring myself another, all the time leafing anxiously through copies of *Newsweek,* looking at pictures of the Tiananmen Square massacre in Beijing.

I knew quite well what was going to happen. I could have left when Dan came back inside. He would have let me go. But instead of standing up when he tapped me on the shoulder, I touched his fingers with the palm of my hand. He sat down on the rug next to me, slid his hand around my neck under my hair, and kissed me. He slipped his palm onto my stomach and rubbed it back and forth across my belly as if he was trying to soothe a tummy ache. There was barely room for his hand to move between my skin and the T-shirt. It was a tiny thing I'd had for years, its weary cotton seams undergoing their final seasonal stretch before I'd have to toss it away.

"Don't do this if you don't want to, Juliet."

It was all he said. Strangely, we were only a few degrees closer now than we had been on the bike. Only this time he was behind me, and all I could do was smell the musty weave of the carpet, as though I had my face buried in the hot fur of a zoo animal, a llama or camel. He was heavy and wet, and he held my hands above my head as the humidity of his breath warmed the back of my neck. I wondered if my label was out. Age 9–12. Wash separately.

It wasn't an unpleasant experience. I was too anesthetized by the wine for it to hurt. On the contrary, I felt absurdly, inappropriately empowered. I liked men, but I'd always been

shy around them. It had never occurred to me before that I
had something they wanted. A trite observation, in retrospect,
but a relative epiphany at sixteen. Frankly, I was young and
naive enough to be flattered. But there ended my involvement
in the situation. I'd be doing this again sometime, and it
would get better. There was plenty of time for things to
become arousing and complicated.

I dressed in silence, unmoved and emotionless as I zipped
my pants and tucked in my shirt.

"That's a pretty top," he said, looking down, tugging at
his fly.

"Thanks," I said, "I've had it forever. Like three years . . ."

Then, to my astonishment, as we knelt together on the
carpet, he covered his eyes and started crying.

"Oh God, Juliet," he gasped, "I'm sorry. I'm so sorry. I
shouldn't have done that to you. I shouldn't have done that."

He was right, of course. He shouldn't have. And he was
damn lucky I didn't tell my dad.

I knew something wasn't right about two weeks before school
started. I would rise later and later in the morning, lan-
guishing until one, sometimes two in the afternoon. Each day
I crawled into the same red shirt and gray sweatpants, scraped
from the floor where I'd dumped them the previous night.
Somehow I was too worn out to pull open my drawers, to look

through my closet and lift something down. Most days I would go without underwear. It didn't seem necessary for lying on the couch or the porch, which was mostly all I did.

Toast crumbs stuck into my feet as I stood on the plastic tiles in the kitchen, holding the fridge door open until my body heat caused it to purr into action. I let it swing closed with a swish, then opened it again, trying to urge myself into the mood for a particular flavor or texture. I reached for a jar of peanut butter, stuck in my finger and licked it off. Then I tore the crust off a piece of bread, bit into it, and threw it in the trash. I lifted a corner of foil from the edge of a plate on the second shelf and slid my pinky through a puddle of solidified grease and barbecue sauce. Nothing tasted right. I picked up one foot and rubbed it against my shin to brush the bits off my sole.

I ought to sweep, then mop, I thought. I ought to brush my hair. I picked up a carton of milk from the fridge, sniffed it, put my lips to the furry cardboard spout, and paused. On the back of the shelf I could see Dad's beer bottles, a couple of Red Stripes and a Heineken. At the sight, the mere thought of alcohol, I weakened my grip on the door and left the kitchen for the bathroom, where I spent the next twenty minutes kneeling by the toilet, looking at the yellowish brown stain beneath the rim, smelling bleach and drains, clay and metal.

After days upon days of lolling around in my increasingly sloppy sweats and T-shirt, I tried going back to ballet. My smart black leotard, snapping fiercely around my rib cage, held me together like a second skin.

"Don't use the barre as a crutch, Juliet," Mrs. Monk said, lifting my hand up from the reassuring wood for a moment. The instant she released my fingers, my palm sprang involuntarily downward to clutch it again. I wondered how I had made it through the week, from my bedroom to the garden, down the street, without it to hold on to. I pictured myself, shuffling from the kitchen to my room only with the aid of a wooden railing, something to grasp and lean into as I dragged my languid torso around the house.

"Concentrate, Juliet, stretch your feet. What's your trouble today?"

Perhaps ballet was for ages 9–12. I had grown up and would now be confined to sitting, talking, a quiet game of cards. I had crossed into an adulthood in which running was reserved for airport departure gates and morning bus stop frenzies, each stride executed under the crippling, ungainly burden of maturity.

The music stopped and the other girls stretched and stalked away in spidery clusters from the barre and into the center of the room. Except me. I stood where I was.

"What's the matter with you, Juliet? Why are you that color?"

Mrs. Monk, the ballet teacher, stood quizzically before me, her hand outstretched, a few feet away. Her voice had taken on a strange, metallic buzz. I could see only her face now. She was up to her neck in swirly black ink and it was closing in around her neck and shoulders. I watched it rise up to cover her skin in splotches, until suddenly the hardwood floor pulled away from beneath me to occupy an entirely different plane, slapping me across the side of the head for good measure.

The indigenous flowers of Northern California were far more plentiful and beautiful than I had ever realized. Until now, my knowledge of local flora stopped with the Golden Poppy. Shameful, really, for the offspring of a couple of proverbial flower children. Just a few weeks before, I had spent hour after barefoot hour prancing about in the unmown meadow of our backyard.

Dad didn't believe in "lawns." The patch of grass out front had once become so long and unruly that a neighbor across the street complained. Their own garden was manicured and sprinkled with such major league precision and regularity that it came to resemble bright green chenille. They wrote us a letter. It threatened legal action if we didn't "get our sociopathic, jungle mentality under control." Dad responded that night by taking a bucket of white paint and writing on the canvas-smooth surface of their lawn: "Stay off my turf." The neighbors then called the police, but by the time they arrived a seasonal February rainstorm had washed away the offending graffiti, and the matter was dropped.

Next time I was out in the hills, I would have to look out for Corn Lily, Monkey Flower, and Elephant Heads. I studied the poster in Doctor Kellerman's office, trying to memorize the shapes and colors of the petals as she withdrew the needle from my arm, pressed a wad of cotton onto my skin, and covered it with a snug bandage. Wild bouquets were a cheering prospect. But it was probably against the law to pick them, anyway.

Doctor Kellerman listened to my back and chest. She took her fingers and applied gentle pressure behind my ears, her face crumpled under her foundation and large plastic glasses. She probed and kneaded me in silence as if she were trying to determine whether I was real or fake. I wondered why she had that shiny, cake-icing layer of flesh-colored makeup all over her face, when there was probably nothing the matter with her actual skin.

"Well, Juliet," she said, "I'd like you to come visit us again in about a week, when I have the results of your blood test. Your urine looks a little dark, but that could be any number of things."

I glanced at the wall, at the rest of the posters. Native Birds of the American West, and to their left, Scoliosis, Seasonal Allergies, Poison Oak, and Head Lice. I sat on the table, its papered surface sticking uncomfortably to my thighs like a toilet seat cover as I buttoned my shirt. I peeled myself free of it and slid to the floor, disappointed that our session was over.

I liked Doctor Kellerman. Had I known earlier how much I welcomed the raw physical attention, I would probably have grown up a whiny, hypochondriac of a child.

"I'm a little concerned," the doctor went on, holding the door open for me, "You're five foot seven, Juliet. How long have you been ninety-seven pounds?"

Out in the waiting room, Dad gave me a quiet, crushing hug. My ribs caved like soggy wicker under the pressure of his great hairy arms.

"Well?" he said.

"She doesn't know yet," I answered. Then, as we walked by the coughing babies and ancient *Redbooks,* past the reception area to the door, I stretched myself tall, put a hand on his shoulder for leverage, and said, "I'm five foot seven!"

Over the next few weeks I grew morbidly familiar with the intricate web of cracks in the ceiling above my bed. Along these changeless, fractured highways, I mapped an entire kingdom. In my mind's eye I would walk around it until I drifted into a feverish sleep, my joints aching as though I really had crossed a particulary nasty terrain.

There was a main road up there, a major artery that ran from one corner of the ceiling to the other. From this stemmed a number of smaller, more irregular veins, whose path my eye would follow to a variety of destinations. Inside my head, I traveled west to the oceans, east to the mountains, south to the desert, and north to the rain. I'd cross the ceiling, falling parched into a dream, awaking drenched. The geography and weather of the landscape above me became one with the temperature of my body. I ceased differentiating between wakeful daydreaming and sleep. One day I woke up and saw a turtle in the bed next to me. Then I awoke again and it was gone. My stomach hurt so much that day I knew I must have eaten him whole.

Sometimes, the ceiling wasn't a map at all. One day, the Pacific Ocean had dried up forever while I slept and I came halfway out of my dream caught in a net. Then the net dissolved and I was free to dive toward the white, cracked mud of the dried-up seabed.

Some days it was a mosaic above me. And sometimes figures and faces. I found my mother up there in the molding around the light fixture, looking down at me from above. Then darkness came, and I lost her, and in the morning I couldn't find her again, only soft bulbs and swirls of white plaster. For several days in a row, in the lower right cluster of fine lines in the paintwork, I designed a geodesic dome. The dome was the most stubborn of my hallucinatory architectures, lingering for days in my peripheral vision, before morphing into a gallows one evening at dusk, then collapsing altogether into abstraction after I got out of bed for a glass of water.

It was hepatitis B. And while the rest of my classmates returned to school to commence their senior year, I stayed in bed and pandered to my increasingly macabre taste in literature. I filled the black holes of loneliness with Zola, Poe, and Hawthorne. Sweating and writhing, stretched out into my boredom or crouched beneath my covers, exhausted by low resistance and latent stomach pain, I dragged my mind across page after page, chapter after chapter of rotting flesh, corruption, deviance, and malady. *Nana, The Fall of the House of Usher, The Scarlet Letter, Therese Raquin.* I ploughed through all of them in some sort of masochistic exorcism by association, all the time expecting my sickness to have flushed itself out each time I closed the book on betrayal, retribution, and forgiveness.

Sometimes I would slip into a half sleep, midsentence, then snap awake, sitting bolt upright, staring at the ceiling, convinced the cracks were shifting like fault lines and the slices of ceiling moving together, ready to implode, crumble, and collapse on top of me. Then, as I swooped into consciousness, they'd melt back together, and I'd fall back to sleep, tendrils of hair wrapped around my neck like curls of ivy choking a tree, or squashed into my face and sticking to my lips and tongue.

Sometimes I would pretend to be asleep when I wasn't. One night, I lay with my eyes closed, listening to Dad move about the kitchen. The suck and swish of the freezer door, the crackle of ice cubes as they tumbled onto the kitchen surface, the metallic click of the whiskey bottle top, the glug of the liquor. Then silence for a moment, as Dad walked into my room and sat on the bottom of my bed. The covers tightened across my feet, binding them to the mattress, its lower corner gently dipping under the weight of his body. We were still experiencing the warmth of a Northern California Indian summer, and I could hear his ice split and fizz in their golden bath of booze.

He sighed, then moved closer to me and took hold of my hand as I held my eyes shut, my face as unrelentingly blank, as neutral and restful as a corpse. Liar, said a voice inside. Wake up. But I didn't. And he took a sip of his drink and started talking to me, the woody scent of his breath drifting over my pillow as he spoke.

"My poor angel," he said, "Oh God. Don't take this little one away from me as well."

Then he was silent, but he stayed in the room at the foot of my bed for a good ten minutes, as I lay there breathing in and out with that deep, snoozey rhythm, pretending to dream.

There were days when I slept all afternoon, then awoke around seven as Dad made dinner, and I'd think it was breakfast and time for school, and comb my brain for forgotten homework. I began to join him in the kitchen for toast or soup. The kitchen chairs had grown cold and hard while I'd been away rolling around in the doughy folds of my hot, saggy bed. I discovered that buttocks had bones. They kneaded their way through my ever-sparse covering of flesh as though trying to plunge through my skin and touch the wood of the seat.

"Eat," Dad commanded, handing me spoonfuls of chocolate pudding or guacamole. "Something fattening. Please, Juliet. Eat."

I managed a slice of bread, half a tomato, and a cup of tea, and returned to bed, intestinal juices squeaking into action, gut gnawing too fiercely on not enough food. And then I rolled over and over in the sheets for hours, wide awake, body clock ticking erratically away in some impossible Southern Hemisphere time zone.

In a tiny, magical peephole of sleep, I had a rancid dream about being coated with salt by a Greek fisherman, left in the sun to dry out, and then thrown onto ice with a pile of fresh squid. I woke in the dark to a buzzing night silence, stumbled over to my dresser, naked, and gazed at my narrow, beige reflection. My collarbone sat above my breasts with all the definition of a crowbar, poking ornately out at my shoulders, like it had been added on as an afterthought. Knee and elbow joints were now the widest part of my limbs.

Then something stirred behind me. I saw it in my bedroom doorway, reflected in the glass. I reached for the string of my dresser lamp and tugged it on. Squinting against the electric glare, I saw him standing at the entrance of my room, arms stretched out over his head, holding the door frame. He wore a green T-shirt with a picture of Chet Baker on it, but it had been messed up by a splatter of bleach so that a jade-white mildewy birthmark of Clorox disfigured Chet's face.

It was Dan.

He dropped his arms by his sides and squeezed his hands into the front pockets of his jeans.

"You've got hepatitis," he said.

"Yeah," I said, "So have you."

I missed seven weeks of school. The season turned over outside my window, the yellow of the fall rolling in through the slots of my Venetian blinds, the sinking October sun drafting its geometry of shadows across my bedspread a little earlier as each day yawned away from me.

Until one Tuesday afternoon, shortly before Dad was due home from work, I lay dreaming of the roller coaster on the Santa Cruz boardwalk. Instead of dipping and diving and hurtling around its old wooden track by the sea, it sped along freeway overpasses and into tunnels of traffic. My car had the handlebars of a motorcycle and a gear down at foot level. In front of me was a man with a green T-shirt, my breasts pressing into his back as we leaned in and out of the curves together. I held on to the leather seat behind me. Then the vehicle began to shake. The road shook. All the trucks and busses, bikes and roller coaster cars around us shook. And I shook, and I woke up and flung my head back to stare at the roadmap on the ceiling.

The ceiling was moving. The bed was moving. The mirror over my dresser was tapping and clicking against the wall, the walls heaving and creaking, as though the whole house was breaking with my fever and shivering in and out of an aching hot chill. Glass crashed in the kitchen, and books thumped from shelves to the floor. I hurled back the covers and sprang into the living room. And then it stopped. I stood with my fingers wrapped around my collarbone. The front door burst inward and Dad flung himself toward me, throwing me onto the couch, squashing me into the cushions with a massive, urgent embrace, as the overhead light shade still swung back and forth on its chain above us.

It was a 6.9 on the Richter scale. Dad found a transistor radio in the bottom drawer of the kitchen cupboard, and for hours we lay curled up in candlelight listening to the crackle of bad news. The epicenter was located about ten miles northeast of Santa Cruz along a segment of the San Andreas Fault, near Loma Prieta in the Santa Cruz Mountains. A thousand landslides had decimated three hundred homes in the hills. Ford's department store, the Coffee Roasting Company, and much of downtown Santa Cruz had fallen in on itself. The stench of natural gas crept across local neighborhoods, water pipes ruptured, phones chirped shrill, alarmist busy signals as arteries were severed or callers jammed the circuits. Houses were wrenched from their foundations. Aftershocks continued to shudder through the body of the earth, agitating impulses, taxing reflexes, vexing raw nerves. Sixty-three people in Northern California were dead.

At midnight I went back to my room and fell face downward on my bed. The next morning I awoke at seven, ripped the sheets from the bed, threw them in the washing machine, and consumed a giant breakfast. Two cinnamon rolls, three eggs, a vegetarian sausage, a piece of wheat toast with honey, and an apple fritter the size of Portugal. I gained ten pounds that week. And on Monday, October 23, I returned to school.

I had missed the Industrial Revolution, *The Canterbury Tales,* Julius Caesar, the endocrine system, and nuclear fusion. I had also, apparently, missed any number of theories and rumors as to my recent whereabouts. Sitting on the sidelines of the volleyball court, waiting to be rotated in, one of my teammates scooted down the bench next to me. She was a sexy, athletic girl with an awesome power serve and surfer's suntan.

Looking soberly toward my shoelaces, she leaned a little closer and whispered.

"Don't worry. I had one too. It's not so bad. It's not like a fully formed baby just falls out of you, all sad and blue."

"Had what?" I asked.

"A miscarriage."

• • •

For some people, the ground beneath their feet is all they ever really come to rely on. When you can't even depend on that not to fall apart on you, all you have is each other.

The boardwalk roller coaster was screaming around its tracks again within two weeks. I made chocolate cakes with a collection of schoolmates and we served them up in some of the makeshift shelters downtown.

I volunteered at a temporary daycare center in a church. I didn't know it then, but it would be the most kind and useful thing I would do for a long time.

I read from a beat-up collection of kids' library books, distracting confused preschoolers with tales of giant turnips, stringless puppets, and shoemaking elves, while their parents picked up the pieces of their lives.

The children's stories were even more morose than the ones I had read when I was ill, only they had pictures to further heighten the ghoulishness of it all, glorious illustrations of the unjust nature of forbidden kingdoms. It was all terribly morbid.

In a room behind a church I started with *Rapunzel,* in which the anemic wife character, standing pale and thin by the window, plea bargains away her firstborn child after her husband snatches a head of lettuce from the witch next door. The child, Rapunzel, grows up in a featureless, illogically doorless redbrick tower, while the witch and a handsome prince alternately yank their way up her long rope of hair to visit.

"How is it, Mama," Rapunzel lets slip one day, "that you feel so much heavier than the prince?"

The flash of the shears, the savage hacking of the hair, the banishing of the prince to the dessert where he wanders around until his thigh-high boots are unfashionably scuffed, his eyes scratched out until he is blind. Then Rapunzel comes to him singing in a ripped-up purple nightgown, and they marry, sightless and shorn, amid great rejoicing.

I read them *The Princess and the Pea,* holding up for the children a picture of the cocky, eligible bachelor prince, clad in white tights and a frilly collar, standing with two greyhounds, archery caddy poised with his master's bow and arrows in the background, as though posing for the cover of a fifteenth-century men's magazine. Money, power, sports. Get the woman you really want. A real princess. And so he works his way through a series of fat, thin, and manic-depressive royal offspring, until an alluring woman in a wet dress shows up one night, dripping on the carpet, claiming to be the genuine article.

And the queen has all the bedclothes taken off the bed. And she puts a pea under the mattress. Then more mattresses, until there are twenty-seven feather beds and twenty-seven mattresses on top of the pea. And on top of that, the real princess sleeps, looking something like a store mannequin tossed onto a stuntman's crash mat.

The children sat quietly in the smelly church hall, contemplating each image, tugging at their underwear, undoing hairdos, wrapping shoelaces around their fingers.

"In the morning she complained to the queen. 'I barely slept a wink. I do not know what was in the bed, but there was something hard in it.'"

One of the older boys sniggered.

"'I'm black and blue all over.'"

It was hard not to laugh myself, selling them this hogwash. Some of the kids were close to eleven or twelve and just a little too old for it.

"'Only a real princess could be as tender as that.'"

I finished the story, and the children talked among themselves about why the pea didn't get squashed.

The tiny, blond girl in the front row asked me, "Why did the prince still marry her if she woke up black?"

Stores were reopened, insurance claims processed. Dan McKenna even opened his small home to a handful of Boulder Creek residents displaced by the quake. Until mid-November, his fancy carpet became a camping ground, a charitable, warm-spirited slumber party for the newly homeless. He stopped by our place one evening to see whether Dad and I would like to join them for a pot roast later that night. Dad contributed a couple of onions and headed over there for an hour or two. I declined. After the earthquake, only things worth rebuilding were repaired. Things that were too shaky to survive were either torn down or simply left alone.

The Trick Shop

In the orderly mesh of streets north of Market and west of Van Ness, the intersection of Geary and Hyde was the absolute balls of the city. I'd moved up there after college, hoping to chase my spirit in the heart of San Francisco, but apparently I could only afford rents in the groin. With a degree in psychology and dance from UC Santa Cruz pressed safely between the heavy pages of *A Pictorial History of the Custom Classic* back home, I moved into a fourth-floor studio apartment in the Tenderloin. But that itching, throbbing, sexy, nasty, irresistible knob of cheap apartments, hotels, bars, all-night grocers, check-cashing centers, and liquor stores was the center of the world to me. I loved it.

My fingers were habitually black with the ink of the free newspapers. I quite often went outside with it all over my face, not realizing. Gerald Ng, the man in Ng's International, the corner store below my place, would stare and then divert his eyes toward the TV behind the counter, as he rang up my double mint gum and my concentrated orange juice.

"You fight with your boyfriend?" he asked me one day.

"No," I said. "No boyfriend to fight."

Other times he would smile, then take a cool suck on his cigarette.

"Two dollars," he'd say. "You paint your apartment?"

I blushed and smiled, until one afternoon I caught sight of my reflection in the metal handle of the store refrigerator, nose and cheeks smeared with the muddy shades of the Bay Guardian classifieds.

"Seventy-five cents. You fix your car today?"

"No," I said, rubbing saliva around my chin and cheekbones. "I'm looking for a job."

It was 1995 and I was twenty-one. I found my dream job on a Saturday afternoon in late January, while lying on my apartment floor, hip bones grinding against the wood, hand slapping the paper back in place as the wind through my open window flipped the pages relentlessly back into the phone sex and strip club section.

The job I wanted lived in a box with a small red headline, neighbored by ten-word rally calls for cocaine addicts, hayfever sufferers, or telemarketers—training available. Recruitment, left and right, for desperate people or lazy people, students, patients, people on the margins of society, anybody looking for some oddball niche, a weekly paycheck, no strings.

"Work from home selling Allied Products. $500+ weekly. Send for brochure." "Suicide hotline seeks volunteers." "Herpes hassles? Get help, get paid." "Dog walkers wanted." "Tattoo Workshop." "Learn Yoga!" "Teach Tarot!" "Stop hair loss now!"

In this bizarre back page marketplace, peddling quick fixes and fast bucks, I found my first official calling as a fully emancipated, able-bodied adult.

I was always, secretly, latently selfish. I disguised it as self-sufficiency, or shyness. But I looked out for myself and stayed out of trouble. It was this social standoffishness that discouraged me from moving into a house shared with roommates when I moved up to the city. I could have found a much nicer place that way. I looked at a few. A majestic Victorian in the Haight, with a musician and a medical student, a piano and two cats and a view of the Panhandle. A flat in the Castro with a couple of gay schoolteachers and a hot tub. I loved the architecture, the furniture, the warmth of the worn-out rugs, the jovial stickers and clippings and photos of nieces and classmates on the fridge.

"We cook risotto every other Thursday."

"But we do have Call Waiting."

"And no music after nine."

"Devon starts his commute at five-thirty."

"All of the movie channels."

"So we split that three ways."

"Full use of the garden."

"None of us smoke."

"All of us smoke."

"We only share milk."

"What do you do?"

My studio was a cold, shallow dive compare to the cozy depths of their homes. But the ceilings were high, and the room had two giant windows facing Cleo's, a bar, and Roland Trading, a food and liquor shop—Ng's competition across the street. I had a double mattress, a shelf full of books, a dresser, and a record player. I had a large orange beanbag cushion, sitting plump and loud in the corner, like a giant citrus. I also had a full-length mirror propped up against the wall. It made the room look bigger. It made me look taller, leaning back at an obtuse angle against the white paintwork.

In my walk-in kitchen I had one of everything. One fork, one knife, one red enamel plate, one red enamel mug, its once white interior now coated in caffeine silt. I did have two glasses. Two matching wineglasses, one with a small chip in it. I planned to take the damaged one, if anyone ever came over. But nobody did.

And in my tiny bathroom, the rest of my personal effects—crusty nail polish, generic hygiene products, and expired pharmaceuticals—lurked undisturbed in a private mess. As well as a shower, I had a tub, and I'd soak in it, quiet and alone.

"Healthy women, 21–30 to become ovum donors. $3,000 plus expenses. Consider an act of love. Give the gift of life!"
Rapt by this prospect of subsidized altruism, I dialed the number. After a click, a warm, female voice came on.

"Thank you for calling the Bay Area Fertility Center. Our office hours are Monday to Friday from nine A.M. to five P.M. If you are responding to an advertisement for ovum donors, please call back during business hours. Or refer to our Web page and online questionnaire at www.BAFC.net.

That afternoon, it seemed like the ticket. I suddenly had to create a life, a bundle of pink, excited flesh, filled with love and potential. I had to give it away before I could get on with even my laundry. I couldn't wait until Monday. I went to the library and fumbled my way through an email registration and remedial Web navigation. The same box continued to pop-up. "Unknown Host."

Eventually I solicited help from a student to my left who knew where on the screen to type in the letters and dots. Within seconds she'd summoned up a pastel and floral background, covered with images of pregnant bellies and newborns. I clicked on a picture of a young college-age woman with jeans and glasses and unruly red hair, shaking hands with an older, more professional, more together couple dressed in suburban casual. Sweaters and makeup and khaki pants. The infertile mother had red hair, too, only hers was combed into a neat bun. For a moment I hesitated. A picture of snide, fairy tale injustice crept into relief on the face of this otherwise wholesome image. The businesslike handshake. The teary thank-yous. The sacrifice. The promise. The pact. At my side, the student looked on.

"What do you think of this imagery?" I asked.

"The resolution could be better," she said. "Looks like they used a low-end scanner."

I clicked through and filled out the form.

Dad called. I told him I'd been interviewing. I found a bar on Geary with a dartboard. I invited Ng's son, Brian, who worked in the corner store three days a week, to play darts with me on Wednesday. Brian was a fashion boy. He had a wet-look, gelled-back haircut and a flashy red Camero, its high-end stereo speakers paid for by my daily soda and muffin purchases. He drank. He smoked. He put cigarettes behind his brittle black hair for later. The bar only had two darts, so we had to walk up and pull out the worst of our two tosses and throw the second dart again. Brian had never played before, but he kicked my ass, even after four beers to my three ginger ales.

"I don't care," I said at the end. "Sign of misspent youth."

"What? Smoking?"

"Being good at darts," I said. "Or pool. Pinball. All bar sports."

"How come you don't drink?" he asked, tipping the final threat of pissy yellow froth down the side of his glass into his mouth.

"It makes me sick. I have a bad liver. I just can't. Even the thought of it . . ."

He just nodded, as though he knew.

"Ever been to China?" I asked.

"I'm American," he said. "My fiancée's Filipino. We're engaged."

"I see."

"I'm in school," he said, quite seriously. "Government. At City College."

"I just graduated," I said. "Santa Cruz. Dance and psychology. Not in that order."

"Dance? And psychology? What can you do with that?"

A week later I returned to the library. After waiting in line for twenty minutes, I sat down at a computer station to check my e-mail. There were two messages. One welcoming me to my new e-mail service, detailing how I might set up my personal address book, send attachments, and check my correspondence from anywhere in the world—though they failed to add that a computer was necessary to do so, thus eliminating the very convenient locations of, say, my bed or the kitchen.

The second message came from "Info@BAFC.net."

"Thank you for your recent inquiry. Your questionnaire indicates an affirmative response to question number:

12c

which we regret disqualifies you from donating ova. Thank you for your interest."

12c was on its own line. 12c was an insertion, stuck in the middle, looking like a typo, but not one. I'd got one wrong. I'd taken the Gift of Life multiple-choice test and flunked. 12c was hepatitis B.

The bathroom ceiling was breaking out in a black-green fuzz, a five o'clock shadow in pestilent mildew creeping out of the damp, creamy paint. I tipped my head back into the water and let it fill my ears and soak my hair, lifting my head, heavy and tangled, only when my chest started to ache from holding my breath. I rubbed my thighs with lavender soap. My skin was yellow. Ochre, it would be labeled in a crayon set. Or Mustard, or Custard, or Crème Brûlée. Not peaches, not ivory or baby pink, but a toxic, nicotine tinge. Tarnished. It was actually the light shade, which was brownish-orange paper, that cast that hue across my skin. I knew that, but all the same.

I discovered for the first time that my upstairs neighbor had a particularly annoying laugh. I could hear him through the tiny bathroom window, whooping and shrieking like a cartoon dog or someone being tickled. Each time I approached the point of melting relaxation in the warmth of the water, I tensed to its hysterical, convulsive peals. I suppose I had never noticed it before, or I'd kept the window closed. Or nothing had been funny since I'd moved in.

It took a full hour to unsnarl my hair. Two plastic combs snapped and catapulted into the mirror. I wrestled vigorously with the tangled curls, struggling to undo knots. But I would never cut it. Perhaps I'd use a more expensive conditioner next time. I sat in my beanbag, prickly between the legs from rubbing myself with the perfumed soap. Aside from that, I felt a little better and made myself some scrambled eggs.

After this I answered an ad that said "Local Color—up to $100 a day cash. Work with professional photographer. Fun modeling opportunities—growing SF attraction. Hippy, gay, drag, bikers wanted. Make cash this week!"

The job was at Fisherman's Wharf, the cheesy seaside zone of the city that existed and subsisted solely by virtue of tourism. For any number of visitors who stayed in the Wharf hotels and spent their days eating crab, saltwater taffy, shopping for cheap sweatshirts, ugly watercolors, and stereos, and gawking at the hopelessly eighties-era silver mime break-dance guy, this was San Francisco. To look around, you'd think the city was economically dependent on the fishing industry, whereas, actually, it was merely dependent on selling the idea of it to foreign travelers. The fact is, the Wharf had nothing to do with the rest of the city. If you were a native, it would be a good place to meet your clandestine lover. There would be absolutely no chance of running into anyone you knew, aunts and cousins from Ohio and Wisconsin not withstanding.

I met with the photographer, whose name was Mario, at his little booth at Pier 39. He was looking for people to pose as hippies, gays, drag queens, and other incarnations of the San Francisco fruit and nut tradition.

"I need a new flower child," Mario said. "My last girl moved back to Montreal. Do you have any tie-dye? Any beads?"

In the background a heavyset German was wriggling around on a bench, flanked on each side by a bearded, blond biker in black chaps and a leather cap, and an Asian boy in high heels, fishnets, and a green velvet miniskirt.

When Mario left me alone for a minute to take their picture, I ran away in terror.

Most people would have taken a regular office job. There was no shortage of sane, white-collar work available for about ten dollars an hour. I could have entered data, answered phones, or filed documents. But I didn't have the clothes. Of course, I could have shopped Savemore or Discount Duds and pulled together quite a variety of fake suits. I could have gotten the clothes. But I didn't want them. And the wind changed. The pages flipped. I answered another calling.

"Healthy, attractive women 21–30 . . ."

And for my next overwrought trick, I became a pastiche of an adult instead of the real thing.

I bought a pink, see-through thong with cartoonish cups of tea on it. It was $4.99 and made in China. I started work the day after my audition, having impressed the manager by finishing my routine sliding into full one hundred and eighty degree splits with my leg up the pole.

"I don't see that very often," he said.

The Cherry Tree was a small, squalid place, operated by a giant, hard-drinking Scot named Keith Macintosh. He squeezed my hand so ferociously my index and little fingers met and crossed in the middle of my hand.

"You'll love it here, love."

Keith Macintosh, I would learn in time, was always right.

If there was one thing I missed about early childhood, it was being permitted to run around with nothing on. Clothing perplexed me for some time as a young girl, and I asked my father and other adults about it quite often, slipping the question furtively in between less embarrassing queries such as "Why can't people fly?" or "How many grains of sand do you think I'm holding in my hand?" I never got the same answer twice. "To stay warm." "To try on a skin of a different color." "To blend in." "To stand out." I suppose I was just too young for the most brutally definitive explanation. I had eventually drawn my own conclusion, of course, in adolescence, when the only explanation came suddenly into hot pink relief.

This was a job that "most" people wouldn't do. Like mining, dressing corpses, becoming a trapeze artist, beekeeper, or stuntman. It was less extreme than any of these, but not without its shock value—a subterranean whiff of daring, a considerable helping of cash and a sizable one of sleaze.

At first I thought I would just work once or twice, on a lark, like pulling some outrageous, once-in-a-lifetime trick-or-treat prank, just to make ends meet until I found a "real job." But it didn't quite happen that way. What happened was this: I made friends, I made money. I liked to perform, I liked to be different, and I liked a large income for part-time work.

It *was* a real job. Like most others it came with its own set of occupational hazards, psychological pitfalls, and plain old bad days. But it was surprisingly easy for me to get into, and surprisingly difficult when it was finally time to get out, because I came to have absolute confidence in my body, yet managed to maintain a rather professional detachment from it at the same time. For a while, it was as if my head and my body were housemates with separate rooms and divergent interests. One was on the night shift, one on the day. It was only when they both came home at the same time that I ran into trouble.

The woman in the dressing room was mixed race with translucent jade eyes and dark hair scrapped into a pom-pom ponytail.

"You're the New Girl," she said. "I'm Jasmine Summers."

I slid my backpack off my shoulder and sat on the stool next to her.

"Well," I said, "with a name like that I'd say you were made for this business."

She didn't laugh.

"Sorry," I said. "What's your real name?"

"That is my real name," she said. "What's yours?"

"Juliet."

Jasmine snorted. "Good luck. We get a lot of Romeos in here."

We put on our makeup in a tiny back room, negotiating for space among an obstacle course of plastic bags, cases of light bulbs, storage boxes filled with office paperwork, unopened packets of kitchen sponges. We drenched our lips in gloss until we looked like we spent our downtime feasting on a backstage buffet of fried food and iced donuts. We drew pouts onto our mouths with lip liner. It was actually possible, with the tiniest upward or downward nuance of the pencil at the edge of the top lip, to blueprint your mood for the entire evening. A half smile, a sultry scowl. We'd rotate a collection of wigs around to maintain the requisite variety of hair colors on the dance floor. Macintosh preferred to keep the full spectrum of blondes, red-heads, brunettes, and Afros on the stages at any given time.

I managed to excuse myself from the wig rotation for the most part. My freaky blond, waist-length, corkscrew curls qualified for borderline "fetish" status, and Mac wasn't one for wasting resources.

With a formidable array of boots lined up beneath our makeup counter, the dressing room resembled some kind of drag army barracks. Everybody wore the highest heels legally available. Four, five, six inches.

"Your arses look greeet in these. Your legs look greeet," Mac would instruct the rookies. "I don't want anyone tip-toeing around barefoot like hippy flower fairies. All right?"

There weren't enough lockers to go around, and items went mysteriously missing on a weekly basis. The mirror was plastered with handwritten notes about possible thefts, their tone often a speculative mixture of accusation and tolerant forgiveness.

"Ladies—I KNOW you love my snake skin cowboy boots, but so do I! Pleeze give them back, no questions asked. Angel."

"Whoever has my red glitter devil horns, you SUCK! If I

just dropped them on stage, I'm an ass. If you picked them up, leave a note on Sunny's locker. Number 15."

Until I had a locker of my own, I wrapped my wallet in my underwear as a deterrent, and stuffed it to the very bottom of my purse. I eyeballed the other dancers and tried to determine who might be the thieving kind. I wondered about the skinny, older one with the ginger hair and the pothole eye sockets. She stood beside me as I stashed my valuables one night, watching in the mirror. I looked into the glass and made eye contact with her reflection.

"You can share my locker until you get your own," she said. "I'll give you the combination."

We didn't even know each other's names and she was standing there naked trying to do me a favor.

"That's OK," I said. "I'm kind of a slob."

She looked skeptically at my neatly folded clothes and my spotless makeup bag, so new it still smelled strongly of fresh plastic, like some kind of sterile baby product.

"Suit yourself," she said, and left the dressing room, shoes in hand, wiping their soles with isopropyl alcohol.

I slid into my teacup lingerie and followed her to the stage.

The silver pole on the club's small, circular rostra, proved a surprisingly practical prop. On my first few nights it was all that kept me from a spectacular death plunge off six vertiginous inches of purple stiletto into a nasty cesspool of beer and nuts and sticky male groin.

I focused a lot on that pole at the beginning. Its clean, silver surface struck me as oddly utilitarian and clinical. It would not have been out of place in a firehouse or a bathroom for the disabled. But it was something to hold on to. I wrapped my legs around it, I rubbed my hips up and down it, I grasped it with both my arms and spun around like a child showing off to her parents on the jungle gym in the playground. I watched the pole like I was afraid it would move, like it would tell me how I was doing. I looked at the pole because I couldn't look at the audience. Until I caught sight of my reflection, my face and body comically distorted in the roundness of its surface. It was like spotting mice on a train track. They're almost impossible to see if you don't know they're there, but once you've seen one, you notice them all the time.

Big hair, sweaty belly, sticky thigh-high boots. "I don't recognize myself!" I wanted to proclaim. But it wasn't true. That was me, all right. After that, I stopped looking, and I made eye contact with customers instead.

I started to play little games to pass the time. With the customers who dressed more casually, I liked to read what was on their T-shirts, to try to determine who they were by what was written across their chest—usually a band, or a place they'd been. Beastie Boys, Judas Priest, or the ambiguous Boston, Kansas, and Nirvana. I'd also crack myself up spotting members of the audience who looked like famous people: Salman Rushdie, Joe Montana, Leonard Cohen, Oliver Stone.

We made all our money in tips, usually in the kitschy tradition of bills down G-strings. We actually couldn't perform fully nude because the club served alcohol, and there was some law about it. We also took shifts as hostesses and sat with the clientele, usually when we had our period and preferred not to spread our legs—although Mac sometimes permitted short shorts "once a month" for stage shows as long as we were topless. It was actually written into the club rules. He was a reasonable sort at heart. He'd lived with women.

I preferred working the stage to sitting down. As a hostess, the point was to hustle for drinks for a cut of the tab. Since I didn't drink, I was denied the pleasure bonus this afforded some of the more lushy girls, who snuck in the occasional illicit cocktail. And most of the punters were tightwads, already hip to the scam, who bought the two-drink minimum and then ogled the stage talent with one hand on their persistently full, warm beer, and the other on their persistently full, warm crotch.

Usually, when we danced for them, they lavished us with praise. And sometimes when we sat with them, they insulted us. The richer and more generous the client, the more aggressively misogynist, it seemed. Especially the young ones. The rumpled old men, the nervous foreign tourists were the more gracious and congenial, relatively speaking.

"Is it all right if I put my arm around you, sweet pea. Is that allowed?" "Here's a little something. Now go buy yourself a nice blouse . . ."

I once sat with a middle-aged doctor from South Beach, Florida, in town for a plastic surgeons' convention, who broke out a wallet-sized collection of his wife and three daughters and proceeded to explain the various enhancements he'd performed on their respective anatomies.

". . . And this is Nicole. Isn't she a doll? And this is Nicole after I did her eyelids. You see how it opens up her eyes? Just like a little doll."

"But she was a doll in the 'before' photo."

He handed me his card. Dr. William Stone, M.D. A.S.P.S. 'Life Is What You Make It!'

"You give me a call in ten years," he said, "and you can still be doing this job when you're fifty!"

"Thanks!" I said, loudly.

It was the young ones who had no manners, the city boys with only a handful of grad-school years on the youngest of us girls, the packs of egomaniacal, wired, tech-industry frat boys, it was they who more often tore into us with a fierce, desperate, motiveless arrogance.

It was the midnineties, and the business and social climate of San Francisco was subtly mutating, with the explosive genesis of the fallacious "new economy," from a center of activism and arts, law, and banking, to a launching pad for self-centered, style-obsessed, rich, spoiled children. I came to hate them, these Jons and Marcs and Zachs and Todds, and I despised their divisive, computer-fixated culture.

They began to command ludicrous salaries, as though part of some exclusive sect who were uniquely privy to the mysteries of an industry in which my own father had worked modestly for years and refused to carry even an electronic organizer. They began to bid for rentals with landlords, offering double the asking price for shoebox apartments, even in my skanky neighborhood, driving real estate prices into fiery orbit, while people on the ground got burned by the hot air from the tailpipe of their high-tech bandwagon.

And then one day a group of boys from BadIdea.com came into The Cherry Tree. They bragged of sixteen-hour days and stock options and their stupid IPO, slamming tequila shots, joking and sneering. I was dancing that night, but I could hear them from the stage. There were four of them. Stupid goatees and rock star leather coats, putting the moves on Sima. She was only young. A tall, pale, blond exchange student from Kazakhstan. She drank heavily, a fact that did not escape the attention of her customers.

"What's the difference between our friend here and a wet T-shirt model?" quipped one of the startup upstarts, squeezing Sima into his armpit. His friends jeered and shook their heads.

"The woman in the wet T-shirt will eventually dry out."

They all snorted and high-fived and said "Dude" for a while.

"So, Reema," said the husky, prematurely balding one, "how do you like your job?"

"It's good," she said, without a smile. Sima was gorgeous, but miserable to talk to sometimes. "I like the money."

"The money? Yeah, that must be pretty good. What do you pull down in here? I'm curious. Really. On the average week. What? One? Two?"

She said something back, but the house disco music had broken into a frenzied, strings-oriented middle section, and I didn't catch it.

The table crackled with snide, staccato laughter.

"Dude," said the one in the retro, horn-rimmed glasses, to nobody in particular, "I make that in day!"

Sima looked on with her usual coolness. She really didn't speak very good English.

On the flip side of the backhanded jibe was the direct hit, the solicitation. This only happened at the tables, and it happened to most of us sooner or later. The house rules on this were quite clear. You said no.

"I have a lot of job-related stress," the man said. "I know you get it. I know this isn't a fun, glamorous job for you. I know that."

"Yeah?" I said. I was surprised by his insight. Most people thought it was.

I'd been at The Cherry Tree about a month. This man, Frank, was a recent regular. Midthirties. Italian. Greek, maybe. Black hair. Moustache. I thought he looked gay. He always came alone, and stood at the back, leaning sadly against the deep, suggestive pink of the club's walls. I'd dragged him off to a corner table that night. Mac was around. "I'm not running a charity, here," he'd said. "Go visit with him, Juliet."

"Have another," I urged. "One for the road."

"I'm driving," Frank said, with an anxious caress of the facial tuft.

"What sort of work do you do?"

"City. City. City work. You know. Downtown," he muttered. "How about you?"

I laughed a short laugh. *How about you?* Cute.

"Look," he said, "if you want to go blow off some steam, I'll be outside in thirty minutes. It'll be worth your while."

"I can't," I said. "Against the rules. Sorry."

"Listen," he said. "You can't get in any trouble with me."

"Sorry."

We closed early that night, for a Friday. Business was dismally slow. It was April 14th, and everybody was home cheating on their taxes instead of out cheating on their wives. I stood in the alley with Mary, one of the veterans, hoping she'd be up for splitting a cab.

Mary was forty. A thin redhead who smoked like a barbecue and worked in a methadone clinic during the day. It was she who had offered me space in her locker, before I even knew her name. She called herself "Flame" in the club. She was the only other girl who could do the splits and I wondered whether she got her fair share of the methadone herself. But she was too upbeat for that.

"Do you want to go dancing somewhere?" she asked me, "It's pretty early."

"Dancing? What were we just doing?"

"That's not dancing" she breathed. "Come on. We've got hours."

"It's two," I said. "I'm spent. I got hit on pretty heavily tonight." As if that had worn me out.

"I'll call you," she chattered. "We'll do it another time."

Mary took my phone number and scribbled it on the back of business card some customer had given her earlier that night. Martin L. Fisher. Director of Client Marketing and Integrated Sales.

"I have a fat address book. Can't carry it around with me. Can I walk you home?"

"Aren't you tired?"

"I don't get tired."

She struggled to light a cigarette, her neon-colored lighter darting around its target as her hand shook in front of her face. Standing there in the dark, illuminated by a tiny lick of orange, her white skin looked like crumpled tissue paper. I'd never noticed before. She smoothed it out pretty well when none of us were around. Proud Mary. Always looking as though she was on to something. Maybe she was.

A woman in a stringy orange coat and white boots wandered past the head of the alley, peered down at us, and moved on.

"I need to talk," Mary continued, a little desperately. "Let me come with you."

We walked up the alley to the main street. Even our doorstep homeless guy was asleep early, curled up on his cardboard near the club's entrance, clutching a purple teddy bear. Looming down on him, high above the door, was a row of plastic-covered glamour shots—interchangeable blondes from the early eighties, none of whom still worked there. Probably none of them ever had. The light bulbs behind the plastic had been switched off for the night, only moderately subduing the screaming fluorescence of their hair and makeup.

"Pretty loud," Mary said with a hoarse chuckle. "I'm surprised he can sleep under that."

On the wall beside the door, painted by hand on the brick in gloss cherry paint, was the club's name, followed by a slogan, in the same fabulous shade. "The Cherry Tree. The Tastiest Girls in Town."

As we walked away, the homeless man began to talk in his sleep. Something about a medicine cabinet and leather sofas. I couldn't really make it out.

Before long, I found myself with enough extra money to purchase some new outfits. I stopped raking through the underwear section of my local Dress For Less and snapped up some XXX rated spandex at Felicia's Fetish down the street from my house. Standard nurse, cop, firefighter garb—butt high, skin tight variations on the daily attire of the people in your neighborhood. The more socially honorable the job, the more likely Felicia would be to trash up the uniform. There was no Loan Shark mini dress, for example, no Claims Adjuster crotchless pantsuit. It was all schoolgirls, sailors, and nuns. Since Mary worked during the day, I often paired up with Sima, who, I soon discovered, had an acute shopping disorder. Perhaps it had something to do with growing up in Kazakhstan.

Felicia's was located in the top half of a split-level unit, above Foot Worship, a monster stiletto boot store patronized mostly by drag queens. I shopped for shoes while Sima climbed the stairs to clatter through rack upon rack of red plastic bras, feather headdresses, and lurid sequined thongs. Down in the footwear underworld I spotted a pair of deep purple platform sandals. The salesperson for shoes had sprinted down to Polk Street for coffee, so I went upstairs and dragged Felicia down to find my size in the stockroom below.

I'd forgotten how much I enjoyed dressing up. As a kid, I'd kept a big wicker hamper of my mother's clothes in the back of my closet. Satin shoes, a Jackie Kennedy pillbox hat with a spotted veil, a handmade patchwork skirt, a suede jacket with tassels. But when I was about seven, my father came into my room to find me striding around, hands on my waist, wearing one of her nylon slips with wads of tissue stuffed down the front to form crinkly, uneven breasts.

He took all the clothes away after that, and gave them to the Saint Vincent De Paul Thrift Shop. About a year later, when Dad and I were in town together Christmas shopping, I saw a young teenage girl, smoking a pipe in the park across from Animal Instinct Pet Emporium. She was wearing the patchwork skirt. She'd shortened it a bit, but it was definitely my mother's skirt. I was going to point it out to him, but he started to show me a parrot in the pet store window, and when I looked around again she was gone.

Sima and I bought Chinese food for lunch. I presented my new shoes over a bowl of hot and sour soup. When I asked what was in her own bag, she reluctantly pulled out a vast and opulent array of Felicia's most stunning and expensive items. Skirts, shirts, bodices, some of them in duplicate styles but different colors. Several hundred dollars' worth of real silk, genuine leather, and hand-sewn rhinestones.

I hooked an emerald satin halter top onto my index finger and twirled it around with a breathy whistle of astonishment.

"Take," she said, pulling from her bag a deep blue version of the same item. "I don't want."

Perhaps she was breaking Mac's patriarchal rules and

making a little money on the side, after hours. Perhaps I was the only one who wasn't.

I often left The Cherry Tree alone. There was so much light and noise on Broadway that I never found the neighborhood particularly menacing or unsafe. It was the collective cheer of the late-night party crowds that troubled me more than anything, their concerted festivity an unwelcome affront to my psyche five minutes after I'd clocked out. I usually hailed a taxi as soon as I could.

One night, when I was desperately tired and cranky and not in the mood to wait around, I started to walk, hoping to flag down the first cab that came along. Instead I found myself moving stubbornly into darker and quieter streets until there was little traffic of any kind.

As I trudged further from the voices, the music and neon signs, I realized that I was being followed. I could hear the unflagging rhythm of footsteps behind me in the distance, their pace increasing with mine, trying to catch up. I turned to look but it was too dark to see. With a vengeance, I began to measure two sidewalk slabs per stride instead of one. At the corner of Taylor and California Street, I stopped at a pay phone, wondering whether I could call a cab company to come to the intersection. I reached into my purse for my wallet and found nothing but keys, my sunglasses case, and a tin of Astrotacs, the intolerably strong mints.

I looked back down the street, swallowing such a large helping of rage it felt as though I had a tennis ball stuck in my throat, trying to decide whether to return to the club and create a giant billboard in angry, red lipstick on the dressing room mirror.

"Maybe I'm crazy, but if you pocketed my—"

And there I saw the source of the manic footsteps, a slim, female figure galloping out of the darkness towards me.

"Flame?"

"Flame? Flame? Don't use that name out here . . . it's way past closing time. For God's sake call me Mary."

She reached out and handed me my wallet. "You dropped this in the doorway," she said. "I've been chasing you for ten blocks!"

"Why didn't you say something? I would have stopped."

"I dunno. I guess I didn't want a lot of noise. There's all kinds of cops around at this hour. I try to stay out of their way."

"Jesus," I said. "I thought I was about to get mugged!"

"Quite the opposite," Mary said. "Can't say I blame you, though. Malice is the norm, and all that."

I hesitated before returning the wallet to my purse, wondering if I should give her some kind of reward.

"Don't worry," she said, watching my fingers pinching at the clasp. "It's all there."

"Thanks for returning it," I said.

"Thanks? Thanks? Of course! We rip our customers off

for money, not each other!" She let out a wicked laugh. "Pay no attention to those signs in the dressing room. People leave their crap all over town and then try to blame each other."

"Thanks," I said again. "This means a lot. I'll remember this."

"Yeah," she said. "You will. You'll leave your crap all over town, but you'll only have yourself to blame."

Mary walked me all the way home. I asked her in, somehow thinking we'd curl up on my mattress like summer camp pals, drinking warm milk from my matching glasses. But she said she had to go home.

I took a sip of water from my unchipped wineglass. And just before flopping into bed at 3:30 A.M., I looked out of my window to see Mary drinking coffee in the all-night diner across the street, apparently engaged in a lively conversation with the Mexican cook behind the counter. There she was, still going, in the well-lit window, like some kind of degenerate vigilante superhero who never sleeps.

She wasn't bad in a crisis, either, as it turned out. God knows, we'd have our share of them.

San Francisco was just too small a city. At first, after Santa Cruz, it had felt like an expansive, cosmopolitan World Capital. Cathedrals, parks, suspension bridges, and great big banks. But as it wore on me, it shrank to fit around me. It was just an oversized, overly decadent town. Not a city at all. You could walk almost anywhere you wanted to go in an hour or less. Drive anywhere in a cab in five or ten—as long as it was before three in the afternoon or after one in the morning, which in my case it usually was.

I was breaking in my purple sandals. Jasmine was on tables, tangled alone in the gluttonous limbs and torsos of a high-proof bachelor party.

"Take it off!" a youthful Asian boy in a tuxedo yelled repeatedly at Jasmine, beer and vodka bleeding from the corners of his mouth. "Take it off!"

"*She's* taking it off," Jasmine explained.

I had my back to them, scooping my body back and forth relentlessly in a low, smiley arc.

"Take it off," said one of the friends. "C'mon. He's getting married on Saturday."

I uncoiled myself from around the pole to face them and locked eyes with the groom-to-be. The moment he saw my face, his mouth heaved itself into a gaping oval, threads of saliva stretching from top lip to bottom. He pounded the air with his fist, alcoholic tears juicing from the corners of his pink, weary eyes.

"All right, Juliet," he hollered. "Right on!"

It was Brian Ng, from the corner store. My darts partner. The owner's son.

"Get 'em off!" he wailed, although I had nothing on. So I took off my shoes.

He was there the next day, shrouded in a smirk and a hangover behind the counter at Ng's market in the early afternoon. I placed a small milk and a low-fat lemon yogurt on the counter and reached for my purse.

"Don't worry about it," he said.

"Come on," I said, handing him the same twenty he'd slotted into my G-string the previous night.

"You look different. At your office. I mean," he stammered. "At your job."

"You looked different at my office, too," I said.

He counted out my change in a visibly nauseated stupor, and I turned to go.

"So at least you found something to do with the dance and psychology," he said.

"I'll never get a straight job," Mary breathed in a toasty voice, peeling her boots off after a long night of sidestepping mustachioed advances from the ever-predatory Frank.

"What about the clinic?" I asked.

"*Heroin addicts?*" she squeaked, as if she'd just discovered a couple of them stuck to the bottom of her shoe. "They don't count!"

Mary, it had turned out, was a qualified nurse. It was the one stripper uniform to which she took offense. "Fucking degrading," she'd hiss every night after I tore apart the Velcro on the starchy white mini dress.

"How can you work a day job?" I asked her, stepping into my jeans. "When do you sleep?"

The woman in the orange coat was hanging around on the corner of Broadway and Romolo Place again, anxiously feeding her hoopy earring around and around in circles through her ear, talking all the time on a cell phone. She eyed us expressionlessly as we ducked into our cab and pulled away. In the taxi's rearview mirror I saw her push the sharp, black aerial of her phone back into its little plastic body. She pressed her index finger and thumb into the corners of her eyes for a moment, stuffed the phone into her purse, pulled the strap of her flimsy gold sandal back over her heel. I watched her from the safety of the cab's backseat, staying on her solitary figure as she became smaller and smaller in the tiny rectangle of glass. She just stood there alone in the dark, waiting. It was like watching a slasher movie from the quiet comfort of the living room sofa. And then she faded away, and I dropped uncontrollably into a cold half sleep.

I went home with Mary that night. She lived in a cavernous, rent-controlled Victorian in the Mission district, with a male housemate. The couch was a suede, donuty sort of sofa, the type of furniture you'd normally want to recline in, to sink back into. But Mary and I were on the edge, tentative and rigid and angled forward, racers in some unidentified sport, nervously anticipating the starting pistol. Before us on the marble coffee table were a stack of weekly newsmagazines, a cropped drinking straw, and four neat lines of shimmery white dust.

"I do it for the money," Mary chattered with short, bitter sniff. "Not the dancing. The methadone clinic. I was doing just the club five nights a week. It was fine at first. Maybe for the first eight or ten months. Like being part of the circus. All that blinding glitter and no one can take their eyes off you."

I nodded. I swallowed a liquid metal swallow. I was feeling mighty agreeable. She could have said it was like mining gypsum in Siberia and I would have beamed in affirmation.

"But then it got boring. Night after night, the same routine gyrations, the same bunch of drunks and leches. The empty seduction. Pretty soon, I couldn't do it unless I was buzzed. And then, of course, I needed another job to subsidize my other job—you know what I mean? So I started nursing again, at the rehab clinic."

Mary was a beauty. I wished I'd met her sooner and hoped I'd know her forever. She glanced toward the table.

"Shall we?"

I sucked excitedly on my teeth.

"Five more minutes," I said.

"Five minutes?" she spat back, as if we wouldn't live that long.

Mary bundled her thick red hair into her hands, dived forward and up again, knocking her head back with a crazy gasp.

"Does your housemate mind?" I asked.

"T-Bone? He better not. He's the one who gets it for me."

"T-Bone? Male stripper, is he?"

"He's a PE teacher, actually."

"What's his real name?"

"Oh, I don't know. Something dorky."

"What could be more dorky than T-Bone?"

Mary sucked in her cheeks, not answering, and passed me the straw.

The powder hit the space between my eyes with a caustic smack. I winced at the momentary jab behind my left eye, tugged at my incisors with my lips and tongue and then swallowed another steely blade of saliva.

We talked. And then we talked some more. And then we *really* talked. About Mary's childhood in Detroit, where she had wanted to become an ice skater, about nursing, and needle exchange programs, and how sad were the lives of junkies and lonely old men.

"Mind you, I'd be out of a job without them," she said.

"You'd be out of two jobs," I pointed out.

Mary laughed. Mary ruled the world. We *both* ruled the world. I told her about my mom, and my father and my liver. And when I'd finished I stared down at the shiny black and white swirls of the marble, and it all looked terribly flat.

"You can always drink yourself down if it gets too much," Mary suggested, lapsing into a suitably gentle bedside manner. "I've got a ton of booze in the house."

"I don't drink," I sniffed. "Remember?"

"Oh, yeah. I forgot."

I leaned forward and reached for one of the newspapers on the coffee table.

"*Washington Post?*

"It's the Unabomber issue," Mary said. "The Manifesto."

I thumbed it open and began to scan the dense paragraphs of sociopolitical diatribe.

"*Almost everyone will agree that we live in a deeply troubled society.* Well, he got that right. What else?"

"He goes on to defend the use of the word 'chick.'" Mary pressed her chin into my shoulder and read with me.

"Here it is," I said, pointing to paragraph 11 of 230. "*Broad and chick are merely the feminine equivalents of guy, dude and fellow.* Damn right. What's wrong with 'chick'?"

"I like 'chick.'"

"*Feminists are desperately anxious to prove that they are as strong and capable as men. Clearly they are nagged by a fear that women may NOT be as strong and capable as men.*"

"What?" coughed Mary, clawing at the pages. "Where?" Her eyes hovered all over the place. "This thing's full of typos. Could've used a round of spell check if you ask me."

"*Art forms that appeal to modern leftist intellectuals tend to focus on sordidness, defeat and despair. Or else they take an orgiastic tone, throwing off rational control as if there were no hope of accomplishing anything through rational calculation and all that was left was to immerse oneself in the sensations of the moment.*"

"What? I don't agree with that one bit."

"Yeah. What's wrong with an orgiastic tone? Bastard. Let's hope they catch him soon."

I dragged my finger through the snowy film on the surface of the table.

"I can't believe you get your coke from a PE teacher," I said.

"Oh, it's not *coke,*" Mary said. "It's *speed.*"

It wasn't long before Mary didn't rule the world at all. Until there was no world worth ruling. Just my own agitated heart trying to thump its way out from between my lungs. I walked home at five A.M. To my disgust, the morning commute had started, and well-groomed, fresh-faced day people sped past me in cars, drinking coffee, *coffee* to wake up, talking on cell phones to other awake, responsible people.

I was all ready to start something, but everything was finished. I made hot chocolate with whipped cream, but it wasn't exciting enough to drink. At noon, I clawed my way into a wretched, guilty sleep.

The most logical conclusion to this incident would have been for me to incarcerate all white-powdered stimulants in the same untouchable mental vault in which I held alcohol. To swear it off forever just as I had sworn off wine, beer, computers, and male tech workers. I had, after all, formed all my other prejudices quite swiftly and with unyielding, Chauvinistic ease. But I fell into a vicious pattern of alternative artificial stimulation and heavyweight exhaustion. And for a the entire summer, life flitted predictably between manic shopping excursions with Sima, frenzied nights at The Cherry Tree, chattering late-night bonding sessions with Mary, followed by a long and burdensome state of near comatose sleep and depression in my unmade bed.

And then the structure of my days snapped at twin pressure points, and when I pieced things back together again, life was a different shape entirely.

I was standing in the shampoo aisle, scrutinizing the overwhelming selection of plump, plastic bottles. I needed something that would relax my hair so that I could fit it under my

latest wig, a shiny black bob. I had lingered for twenty con-
spicuous minutes and figured I ought to settle on something
and buy it before somebody called security.

Sima, meanwhile, was in nail polish, weighing Rhinestone
Frost against Platinum, Mulberry against Strawberry against
Blackberry Wine. She had unscrewed the bottles and was
painting fruity or metallic stripes on alternating nails,
making faces.

"I'll meet you outside," I said, tugging on her ponytail.

Sima spread her fingers and held her hand at arm's length,
screwing up her chalky, made-up face.

"I don't like," she muttered.

I stared idly at the alarm clocks and bathroom products in
the drugstore window. Ninety-nine cents for a lifetime's supply
of generic hand lotion. Some things were just a good deal. I
waited in the cold. Gray wet puffs of fog tumbled down California Street from the ocean. I wondered why they bothered
with the elaborate display of sunscreen in San Francisco's bitter,
cloudy July. Probably some uninformed management decision
out of Corporate in Minneapolis. In the glass, I could see that
the chain clothing store across the street offered a kaleidoscopic
arrangement of little pink and white T-shirts and cutoff denim
shorts. The thermometer above the bank, with unknowing stupidity, flashed forty-seven degrees in neon green.

And then I stopped staring at the buildings reflected in the
window and looked through the glass again. A small crowd

had formed beside the redundant SPF 50 and aloe creams near the door.

"Ma'am. Ma'am . . . Ma'AM," a uniformed man repeated in an abrasive crescendo. "MA'AM. I'm going to have to ask you to calm down."

I stalked back into the store.

"Step aside," barked the security guard. And I stood frozen by the bronzing lotions as he proceeded to lift Sima's fake angora sweater and tug at the elastic waist of her skirt. He pulled out a cheap umbrella and a pair of flesh-colored knee highs; a dollar forty-nine, on sale.

Sima's dad drove to the store and picked her up. Her *father.* He parked in the bus stop, while her mother and three sisters waited in the car.

"She's only nineteen," he bellowed. "Nineteen!" as much directed toward Sima herself as the hapless drugstore staff. Then, grasping her forcefully at the crook of the elbow, he launched into a terrifying stream of abuse in Russian and pulled her out of the store. Sima didn't acknowledge me. She looked toward her mother in the car and started to cry. Her father threw her on top of her sisters in the backseat, slammed the door, narrowly missing her leg, and drove off.

I never saw her again.

Almost a year had slipped by. With each passing month our

bachelor party crowds yelled at each other over different sports, chose different drinks. Hockey had turned to base-ball, baseball turned to football, warm stout to cold lager, Irish coffees to Margaritas. Nobody knew why. Typically, the metropolitan counter-climate had gone from a sixty-one-degree winter to a fifty-nine-degree summer—with only the cursory respite of a fleeting, eighty-five-degree spring that lasted approximately six hours one afternoon in April. Yet, obedient to the irrelevant tradition of the so-called seasons, the cocktail menu rotated cheerfully on. It didn't matter who they rooted for or what they ordered anyway. All the sports pissed them off the more they talked about them and all the drinks got them drunk the more they drank. It was all the same.

"How much for a little vitamin O?"

It was an older man with a beard this time. I didn't catch his name. He reminded me of my high school geometry teacher. Gingery hair, pinhole eyes so small and recessive they were almost impossible to find on his face.

"I can't."

"You have to say that, don't you?"

"Yes."

"But you're halfway there. See that?" he said, pointing to his partially drunk martini. "Half empty? Or half full?"

But before I could answer, I'd accidentally elbowed the glass from the edge of the table into his lap.

I pressed a napkin into his crotch.

"Two hundred dollars?" he asked, looking at me with his nothing eyes, his nameless face. All right, I said inwardly. Life is short, I told myself. Or even if it wasn't it was a good enough excuse for doing things you weren't supposed to do.

I was too excitable that night. I would have been excited by anything. My horoscope, a cocktail umbrella, a picture of his dog. I wasn't excited by this man, or by the two hundred dollars. I had been so unexcited an hour ago, in fact, that I'd keyed myself up like a windup toy with a huge line of speed I'd bought from Mary for fifteen dollars.

At closing time, I got into his car with him. We drove down Geary Street and he pulled into the Days Inn motel just a few blocks from my apartment. I pretended to look at fliers for local tourist attractions in the lobby while the man checked in.

"We have an activities desk open from nine to four," said the clerk from behind the counter.

"Thanks," I said. "Maybe we'll do the walking tour of Historic North Beach."

My bearded guy kept his head down the whole time, filling out the paperwork. Name, automobile registration, credit card.

"Address, sir?" said the hotel clerk, handing him back the incomplete slip of paper.

He scribbled something onto the form. The man at the desk laughed a little.

"Just up the street," he noted with a smirk. "Same zip code."

He stood in the bath and washed off his feet while I lay on the bed, trying to tune in the radio. It wasn't a very good one, and I had to stop on classic rock. It was the only thing that came in without static.

He took me on my stomach so that we didn't have to look at each other. I pressed my face into the cleanest sheets I'd seen in a long time. Cool, crisp, exciting fresh linen. The man on my back kept saying things to me, whispering and sighing, but I wasn't really listening. I was listening to ZZ Top and Lynyrd Skynyrd. I kind of liked them, really. We'd had an album with this song, at home.

He gave me ten twenty-dollar bills and offered me a ride. I pointed out the window.

"Thanks." I said. "I can see my place from here."

He fell silent for a minute.

"Do you mind if I ask you something?"

"Go ahead," I said.

"Was that your first time doing this?"

"Second."

"Second time for money?"

"No. Second time ever."

He looked out the window, not saying anything for a while but staring in the precise direction of my bedroom window. Then he shook his messy head and puffed a short, breathy laugh.

"Do yourself a favor," he said. "Don't tell any more strange men where you live."

It was my own bed that was dirty. I hadn't changed the sheets in weeks. My jaw ached. I thought I had mumps and looked it up in my medical encyclopedia to see if you could get it twice. I looked up some other diseases just to pass the time. Gallstones and strep throat. And then I just lay there, teeth clenched, waiting.

In the morning my upstairs neighbor started to laugh. Perhaps he had company or had turned on the television, or had just read the funnies. Even with wads of paper towel in my ears, I could hear him through the ceiling, yelping and hooting obscenely as I lay wide awake on my bed with a raw throat. I wondered what could possibly be so funny that early in the day. Certainly not the morning news. Not comic strips. Not people. Yet still he hiccupped away in giddy delirium until I was just about ready to go up there and tear his head off.

The phone woke me in the midafternoon.

"Love? Juliet?"

"Dad?"

"*Dad?* Let's not get carried away, luvvie."

It was Keith Macintosh, from the club.

"I need to talk to you, love." He spoke with an uncharacteristically awful could-I-see-you-in-my-office gravity.

"I know," I said.

"You know? Typical. Always the last to know, bloody management. I'll need you to come in tonight. Time and a half. I know she'd do it for you."

It was Jasmine Summers. She was having what we called among ourselves a Family Emergency—a member of her close family had arrived in town unexpectedly and she would have to lull them with sight-seeing and smooth talk of her steady job at the bed and breakfast, cocktail lounge, or brokerage clearinghouse. I would have to cover her shift on my one night off.

For the first time in months, I took the bus to work that night, instead of walking. It was half empty and I sat in the handicapped seat at the front.

It was true. Jasmine would have done it for me. She was one of the pleasant, responsible ones. Most of the club dancers were. Honest, clean, intelligent, friendly women. Not all strippers were speed addicts and shoplifters. Just the two who happened to become my closest friends. Most of our customers didn't hit on us. I even met huge groups of computer industry people who were well mannered and fun. Big tippers. Courteous and respectful of women.

"You don't have to wade around in the muck," Macintosh had said to me once, when I'd showed up for work looking particulary hard and nasty. "You want to pull your finger out, Juliet."

He was right. I could really wallow in it.

As the bus jerked and hissed through town, I started to read the newspaper of the woman sitting opposite. Something on the front page caught my eye. A mug shot in the upper right-hand corner. A youngish, dark-haired man with a mustache.

"S.F. Officer Arrested after Shift for Soliciting North Beach Vice Cop."

Leaning forward, squinting, I read on.

"A San Francisco police officer was arrested after he attempted to solicit a sexual act from a colleague posing under cover as a prostitute in North Beach.

Frank Henry Arago was cited on suspicion of soliciting prostitution and will appear in court on October 24. The undercover officer said that Arago approached her on foot at the corner of Romolo Place, off Broadway, and offered her $50 for oral sex before he was taken into custody."

It was our Frank. Greek Italian Gay Straight Frank. I should have just taken care of him myself. He'd still have his job, poor bastard.

"He's a very competent, loyal, hardworking officer," said Station Captain Ray Denton. "He's a high performer and in his five years as a patrol officer, Frank has never been in trouble before."

Well, Frank. There's a first time for everything.

The woman folded up her newspaper and slotted it beneath her arm. She was riding with her young daughter next to her, a runny-nosed child of six or seven who had been trying to decipher an adjacent story about the search for the Unabomber, her curious fingers tracing an invisible outline around the black-and-white sketch of the Mariachi man in the hooded sweatshirt that appeared with every article. The girl sniffed and wiped a shiny, wet ribbon across her crusty little lip. Her mother took a tissue from her purse and held it up to the child's nose.

"Blow?"

The bus lurched to a stop. Staring wearily across at them, I sniffed, too. And then I sneezed. I sneezed a nasty wet mess of mucus laced with threads of blood and old speed and caught it in my bare hand where it formed a sticky, silvery web between my fingers.

The little girl laughed at me.

"That lady's got a cold, too," she to her mother.

At the end of my shift, as I left the club, I gave one of my twenties to the homeless man with the teddy bear. I wanted it to be one of the bills from the night before, one of the crisp ones from the guy at the Days Inn. But now I couldn't tell his money apart from that night's tips. It all looked the same in the dark. It was an empty, showy gesture, anyway. One that made me feel better, not him. He'd still be there tomorrow. We both would. I wiped my nose on my sleeve and looked up the street. The woman in the orange coat was gone, of course.

As I turned to leave, I noticed somebody had graffitied our building. They'd messed with our sign in deep blue spray paint. On the part that had read "The Tastiest Girls In Town," they'd changed the "T" to an "N."

"The Cherry Tree," the sign said now. "The Nastiest Girls In Town."

Twenty-seven Mattresses

Jasmine did return the favor. Dad came up to the city for a semiconductor conference and stayed for Thanksgiving. I hadn't been back to Santa Cruz once since moving to San Francisco in January, and Dad had not come to visit me.

"You don't want a bearded old man hanging around," he'd say on the phone. I wondered what that meant. I don't know why he didn't come. But when I opened my door to him that sunny Wednesday in late November, I threw my arms around him and held him with such desperation it was as though I'd been taken from him at birth and reunited that afternoon.

He stumbled and stepped back, his motorcycle helmet slipping from his hand and crashing to the floor where it rolled around in the hallway.

"Come in!" I screamed, "This is my place. I vacuumed."

He stepped inside as I raced over to the fridge and flung open its door to reveal an abundance of sodas and beer.

"Drink?" I asked, "Beer?"

But he wasn't looking at the beverage selection or the dust-free floors. He was looking at me. I let go of the fridge handle and the door swung closed, the room darkening, the beer shivering inside.

"What?" I said, glancing down at myself to make sure I was dressed.

"You look different," he said. "Are you—?"

"Am I what? Different? Probably."

"I hadn't finished," he went on calmly. "Are you all right?"

I looked at him for a moment. Dad hadn't changed at all, hadn't so much as changed his clothes, it seemed, since he waved goodbye to me at the bus station eleven months ago. His hair had grown an inch, and a few more white filaments were now scattered here and there in the coarse brown shag of his beard.

"I can't believe you haven't cut your hair," I said with a shaky laugh.

"You seem a little nervous," he said, not moving. "You don't have some awful news or something, do you?"

"Not—no," I said.

"Not no?" he repeated, "Not no. Different from no, for sure. More like yes, I think."

It seemed he was looking through my clothes, and beneath

them could see a leather G-string and a pair of gold tassels and wads of bills all over me, stuffed under stretches elastic.

Then he backed off, sat down, and glanced around the room with a quiet smile.

"No TV," he observed, nodding.

We split a lime soda and sat together, me on my bed, Dad flopped into my beanbag. We talked for hours about my work with a local dance company, my part-time job at a city bar, about his projects at National Semiconductor and the speech he had prepared for the conference. And all the while in another part of town, Jasmine gyrated in my place and talked with men my father's age, in town for the same conference, who would listen to his very speech on silicon carbide, with a mild headache, the next day.

I stayed in Dad's hotel. Not with him. We traded. He slept in my studio apartment and he offered me the luxury of his room at the Marriot where the conference was being held.

"Take it," he said, "Give yourself a break!"

While he was out getting coffee at Ng's, I pulled my stripper garb from the hangers and drawers, stuffed it in the kitchen closet on top of the vacuum cleaner and the ironing board, and padlocked the door.

"Maybe we can have a soda one night at that bar of yours," he suggested, as the cab rolled up to take me to the hotel.

"I never go there when I'm off duty," I said with a swift smile and a shake of the head.

I pulled shut the heavy taxi door. I could still see Dad in my peripheral vision, standing outside the building, eyeing me like a deep-cover cop.

"Where to?" the driver asked.

But Dad crept forward and stood by the window, miming circles with his hand. I wound down the window. He opened his mouth, closed it, and then stepped backward out of the gutter onto the sidewalk again, as the cab pulled off into the road.

"Hey, Juliet!" he shouted from the pavement. The driver slammed his foot to the floor, sending me crashing forward toward the front seat. "Behave yourself. No TV!"

The clerk at the check-in desk smiled a little when he saw my address. Smug, privileged bunch, hotel staff. Probably made an extra thirty grand a year in bribes alone.

"I'm here for the conference," I said.

I picked up the schedule in the lobby and found my father's talk listed for 3 P.M. the following afternoon, alongside similar panels on Operational Amplifiers, Nitride Bulk, and X-Ray Diffractometry in Wide Band Gap Semiconductors. Passing by the activities desk on the way to the elevator, I noticed they offered the same Historic North Beach Walking Tour I'd found at the Days Inn. I pulled out a couple of fliers about the San Francisco Zoo featuring a pair of new baby alligators. I'd done enough walking around in historic North Beach.

"So which is it?" said the man in the Hawaiian shirt, "Underage or pregnant?"

"I don't get it," I said.

He nodded toward my soda. "I noticed you're not drinking."

"I don't drink."

"Don't drink," said the man, stirring his gin and tonic, "What are you doing in the bar?"

Good question.

"Watching the game," I answered, glancing in the direction of the red and green flashes of Monday night football bursting out of the TV on the wall in the corner.

"I don't know how you can stand it," he said.

"Yeah," I nodded. "It's like the commentary's been tampered with by some closed-captioned saboteur."

He looked at me for a moment, sipped his drink, smiled, and nodded.

"Who's playing?" he asked.

"Ah . . . the Niners and the White—Red Sox? The Warriors and the Mets?"

The man wheezed with laughter, tipping the rest of his cocktail into his mouth and smacking the empty glass back onto the bar with a Hollywood flourish. His arms were thick with hair, smooth, flat crisscrossed strands so deep and dense I couldn't see his skin beneath.

"Yeah, I know. I could use some of it on my head," he said, staring me flatly in the face. "What do you want?"

"Nothing," I answered, staring squarely back.

"I mean what are you drinking?"

"Oh. Coke."

He ordered us another round.

"What brings you to San Francisco?" I asked.

"Optoelectronic Technology. You?"

"High Voltage Diodes."

"Yup," said the man, crunching aggressively on an ice cube. "I had a feeling you were here for the conference."

He leaned in toward me. I could see the contact lenses floating around on his dark brown pupils.

"And what brings you down to the hotel bar?" he asked me again.

"I already told you. I'm watching the game."

"Something wrong with the TV in your room?"

He had me. Or I had him. It wasn't clear.

"I—didn't notice there was one?" I answered in the form of a question, my eyes rolling to the left and right as though looking for stage directions from the wings.

"It looks like a cabinet," he said. "You have to slide back the doors. If you're interested, I'll come up and show you."

In the elevator he rubbed his hands together, smiled, and blew air out of his cheeks.

He said, "I wasn't sure, at first."

"Neither was I," I answered back.

"It's all right," he said, as the door opened to the quite walls and the fire extinguisher and the pristine carpet. "I'm not a cop."

He gave me a hundred dollars. A fifty, two twenties, and a ten. I was getting cheaper. I rolled up the bills, stuffed them into the pocket of the complimentary white terry cloth robe, as I stood in the doorway and kissed him good-bye in the jagged light that cut across our faces from the hotel bathroom. As our lips came apart and he stepped away, I noticed a man entering the room next to mine, head down, fumbling with his key card, yellow plastic binder about to fall from his grip. He wore a name tag, obscured by his arm as he struggled with the lock. The door clicked open and his papers fell to the ground, as the hairy guy walked from my room toward the elevator.

"Thanks, Juliet," called the stranger, sauntering off.

"*Juliet?*" The man next to me looked up, slotting diagrams of board-level components, chips, and circuits between the clumsy flaps of the binder. I stood in silence as he slid his key card into his breast pocket next to his ball-point pen and his hand-sharpened pencil. Below it was his name card.

Dan McKenna.

I fell back into the room and drew the chain across the

door. Then I dived onto the bed, watched the television for four hours straight, and put my money away. I could only find fifty. I plunged my hand into every fold and furrow of the robe but found only lint and a card with prices for the in-house laundry and dry cleaning service. Seventy-five dollars for suits, fifteen for shirts only.

At seven in the morning I awoke to a clock-radio blast of music and a maternal voice selling me waterproof bandages in assorted colors.

Dad's voice was unrecognizable, rolling across the room in amplified waves with a command I didn't recognize, an authority he'd never used on me. He spoke another language, standing on the podium in his rumpled, white shirt. And after the applause, various combinations of physicists and tech nerds buzzed up to him like groupies, like college students posturing and positioning for the attention of a Nobel Prize winner or best-selling author. So this was SiliconeCarbide and the Beat SiC Bulk Growth Process. If only I'd known. I would have picked a different major and could have been a huge star.

I dived at the door after the first knock. Dad and I had arranged to meet in the hotel bar at six. But when I tore off the chain and poked my face into the hall it was Dan.

"Sorry," he mumbled, looking at the floor. "You dropped this outside your room last night."

I took the fifty-dollar bill between my index and middle finger, slid it quickly from his grasp, and tucked it silently into my back pocket. I looked downward, and the two of us carried on as though we were searching for some loose change on the carpet.

"Thanks," I said, rubbing my bare foot on the taupe fuzz, wiping a dark stripe into its surface. "Yeah, well, don't tell my dad."

"What?" he said, rubbing the furry nap of carpet back the other way, covering my track. "That you watched TV all night?" He shuddered and backed away. "I won't."

And that was the last time I would see Dan McKenna for a very long time.

Dad had his back to the sports, moving his face between my eyes and the screen. Over iced tea in the hotel bar I made fun of his tech talk and his groupies while he mocked my apartment and personal effects.

"What's with all the makeup?" he quizzed me loudly. "You live in a Las Vegas beauty parlor. You own enough lipsticks for a person with fifteen mouths. I just don't understand how the market could exist for more than about two shades. Red and pink."

He shook his head, eyebrows puckering and stretching toward his hairline.

"I don't *wear it,*" I whispered.

"Good. You'll look like you were put together from a kit." He scraped up a handful of pretzels and crammed them into his mouth.

"And the toothpaste. Why don't you have ordinary toothpaste. *Rembrandt?*

"It's whitening toothpaste."

"Rembrandt? Juliet? Have you any idea how horrible teeth must have been in seventeenth-century Holland? Rembrandt? Shouldn't it be called Warhol or something? *Lichtenstein.*"

Behind us, I heard somebody snuff out a short laugh. It was Mr. Hawaiian shirt. He winked at me as I looked over my shoulders, then went back to reading in the paper about the assassination of Yitzhak Rabin.

"And watch your electrical outlets and switches," Dad went on. "Fireworks every time I turned on the kitchen light. That place needs major re-wiring."

"Stop complaining," I said finally. "It was your idea to stay there."

"Sorry," said Dad. "I'm very proud of you, Juliet. Honestly. I'm really proud of you." And he squeezed my arm, pushing my small muscle painfully sideways over the bone. "How's the hotel room?"

"Great! All mod cons!"

"Really? Travel iron?"

I ran into the Hawaiian shirt guy one more time, in the elevator, the next day. We were alone from the tenth floor down to the lobby, staring at the buttons to a glockenspiel instrumental of "I'm Still Standing" by Elton John.

"You don't waste much time, do you," he sneered.

"That was my father," I gasped. "You're disgusting. That was my *dad!*"

But as the doors slid open, he just laughed.

My dad and I ate our Thanksgiving meal in a Tenderloin diner. Eleven dollars for a full turkey dinner and pumpkin pie. It was the best and biggest meal I'd had all year. The manager himself wielded up the sweaty, white plates topped with layer upon layer of meat and slippery cushions of mash potato. He came to each table personally to say hello and refill our chunky brown mugs with coffee. Most of his customers addressed him as Will, and he knew their first names in return. Harry and Paul, Mr. and Mrs. Donovan, Spike, Mr. Wang, Elsie. I felt a little left out.

I almost told Dad that afternoon, what I'd been doing with my time.

"I have something I need to tell you," I was about to say. But before I could do it, he did it to me.

He put down his coffee cup and said, "Juliet, I have something important to tell you."

I preferred it that way around. The diversion. I'd much rather catch a curveball than throw one.

"I'm going to Pakistan. I've been offered a job teaching at a college in Karachi. It's a two-year contract. Dan McKenna's going to keep an eye on the house while I'm away."

If I fumbled at all it was because I was still deciding what to do with my own big speech. It was like it was balled up in my mouth and now I had to spit it out while he wasn't looking, and hide it behind my back.

But he didn't appear to notice. "You remember Dan, don't you?" he said.

That night, my dad rode back to Santa Cruz. And I went home. Ng was closed, all was quiet, the city was dead. I sat upstairs by myself, swollen and sleepy and glowing from hot, rich food and warm liquid. Being full is no fun on your own. You might as well be empty. That night, I would almost have liked to have heard my upstairs neighbor laugh. But even he was gone.

The next morning, waking to the whooshes and beeps of the street cleaning and garbage trucks, I unlocked the kitchen closet. My feather boas and sequined shorts burst out and flopped to the ground like so many props in a magic show. I danced smelling of carpet cleaner and Ajax for at least two weeks after that.

This would have been a good time to get out. I was idling at a traffic light when Dad left me. And after he drove away, I went straight on, as if nothing had happened. And I got much worse, in my own confusing, masochistic way. I thought I could go as deep into the business as I wanted, as long as I could find my way back out. You have to be able to come back.

A gauche, ungainly caricature, a piece of human candy with a sticky, horribly delicate center, I came on to every man I sat with in The Cherry Tree. I chose hostessing over dancing to score clients, and I put the moves on them with an unrehearsed, B movie series of one-liners.

"So where are you from, Julie?"

"It's Juliet. Santa Cruz."

"Ever ride the roller coaster on the boardwalk?"

"Not my style. I take my thrills in bed."

"So you grew up riding motorcycles?"

"Sure. I like things I can straddle. Motorcycles, horses . . . men."

• • •

"You look like a model."

"Yeah? And I don't get out of bed for less than six thousand dollars a day."

"Is that so?"

"Yeah, but I go to bed for less than half that."

After a while, it was like someone else was doing the talking. I was a grotesque ventriloquist's dummy, a cheeky talking doll. Some kind of extreme version of Mae West was speaking the lines or pulling the string. The things that came out of my mouth.

"I used to go to the massage parlor," said the man on the bed next to me. "Then one of the girls stole my wedding ring off my finger. She just slid it off in all that oil. Didn't even feel it."

"That's what you get, you cheating bastard," I thought. "That's rotten," I said.

There were, I soon discovered, a good number of cheap, clean hotels in downtown San Francisco. European-style places with the bathroom down the hall, like the Stratford, or the Hotel Union Square, where I lay on the coarse, gray bedspread with Mr. Three. I read the paper while he showered. A teenager was missing in the East Bay. There was a photograph. She was about fifteen, with long, straight, brown hair, parted in the middle like Joan Baez, and thick eyebrows, unplucked in that sexy Brooke Shields fashion.

There was always a kid missing in some direction of the bay. North, South, East. Never in the heart of the city, where it was supposed to be rough and nasty and dangerous. It was always out in the suburbs, where people had yards and wandered off to play down the road or smoke outside shopping malls. A week had passed and the neighbors, it said, were holding a candlelight vigil. Don't waste your time, I thought, she's dead.

I borrowed his cell phone and checked my messages as the hot water hissed and slammed into the tiles a few feet away. Mr. Four had called and I'd have to run across town to another hotel in less than an hour. Shower man had a permanent, motivational message programmed into the phone to display itself in optimistic green light in between calls. "Trust and Believe In God" it said. I hung up, and out he came, rubbing his hair quite joyfully in that lovely white towel.

I went part time at The Cherry Tree and told Mac I was rehearsing with a contemporary dance company. Making excuses to my strip club boss so that I would be free to do something more raunchy. Now that was a slippery slope.

Many of the girls had left. Mary was doing more nursing, and had become a part-timer like me. Jasmine went back to school. I never saw them anymore. No shopping, no dancing. All the camaraderie was gone. The luster of the job had long since dulled. I only saw men.

There were days and nights when I could still smell one man on me while already in the grip of another. Even after showers and changes and clothes, their scent would linger somewhere and pervade my consciousness from somewhere while I was in line at the post office, or doing laundry, or when my head was buried in the neck of somebody else. It came, I finally realized, from my hair. I didn't wash it every day because I didn't have a blow dryer and it matted up and took too long to dry. And one day I discovered that if I rubbed my ponytail across my nose, it smelled of men's cologne and sometimes their skin. I carried that around with me for days, all those men and their smells on top of my head and around my neck and shoulders.

I used to kiss them, in the beginning. And then somehow I reached a point where I wouldn't even consider that.

I saw so many in a row, I couldn't remember who'd done what to me.

"My head hurts where you pulled my hair."

"I didn't realized I pulled your hair, sweetie. How did I do that? I'm sorry."

"Remember that conversation we had last night about the prison system?"

"That must have been somebody else, darling."

I serviced one of my clients in his car because he said he couldn't afford a motel room. I believed him, too. There was a convention in town and the room rates had gone up. Well, there was always a convention in town. The hoteliers used it as a bartering tool.

It was a pretty old car, a butter yellow mideighties Nissan Sentra. We tipped our seats back as far as they would go to make the experience more bedlike, but it was still a little awkward. Mine reclined almost all the way down, but his, the driver's side, only went to about a hundred and ten degrees, stopping when it hit the child's car seat in the back. I was wearing a particulary linty mohair sweater that night, one that shed fluff like a diseased mammal. Hours after I left him, I wondered if he'd had the presence of mind to pick the puffs of blue from the back of his wife's seat. The next day I had a few bruises on my knees and shins from the gear stick, but I had nobody around me to see them or care about that.

"You're the best sex I ever had." They all said that. And I said it to all of them. So did they say it to everyone, too? Did it just get better and better or were we all a bunch of liars?

But the money was fantastic. The best way to build an enterprise, I discovered, was return business, and word-of-mouth referrals. With scheduled regulars a couple of times a week I could make a lot of money with minimal effort in the most comfortable of surroundings.

I managed to set something up with a businessman I met through a regular at the club. A little, elderly New Yorker named Marty Le Beau, who owned an entire luxury apartment building in Russian Hill. Marty was a bachelor and a playboy, and I'd visit his penthouse on Tuesdays and Fridays from seven to nine. Together we'd read The *New York Times* and he'd gulp his way through a fancy wine collection. Sometimes he'd grill me up some salmon, standing small and naked in his bright metallic kitchen.

Marty was, I discovered, something of a philanthropist, with a room in a school library, and a gallery, and a small theater named after him. He went to the ballet, the symphony, the Museum of Modern Art. He showed me a newspaper picture of himself, dining with movie producers at Cannes.

We always had sex in the living room on the carpet, in between the coffee table and the sofa. I offered to do the dishes once or twice, but the maid came twice a week, he said. Then he'd pay me $350 and put me in a cab.

"Let the old lion take care of you," he'd mutter, like a crumpled, twisted-up uncle, as he pressed the bills into my palm.

"I come here to take care of you," I'd answer, on cue.

Sometimes I wondered what Marty did after I left, all alone up there on his leather chair, waiting to go to his untouched bed. Watch cable. Eat dessert. Make calls to his tax attorney. Were there other women? Did he miss me?

"Can I see you tomorrow?" he'd sometimes say.

"I have commitments."

"I know," he'd reply with a solemn nod of his bald little head, "I know. You're a timeshare."

At that time, everything about San Francisco was inflated like a huge, shiny beach ball, bouncing happily around from person to person, place to place, business to business. Fantastically wealthy, fantastically horny, oddly lonely, and sometime inept entrepreneurs from Silicon Valley or South of Market start-ups gradually became a significant sector of my clientele. They were young. Younger than me, some of them. They made three or four times the money I made, and they were happy and strangely desperate to share it. I became steadily richer in early 1996. I had nothing to do with the money. My rent was $475 a month. I put it away in the bank.

Slowly the city atmosphere changed. What once had been a small Italian dinner for four and a bottle of cheap red wine was now a raging and obnoxious all-night dance party with neon-colored drinks and people with stupid names. I never really joined that party. I was the mousey neighbor, timidly tapping on the door to have the music turned down because some of us do have real jobs, thank you. When your actual job description is "Life of Party" it looks all too much like work.

Contrarily, in my spare time, I'd do conservative things like go to the library. I checked out wholesome or funny books.

Sense and Sensibility. Lucky Jim. I ran into Jasmine reading *Film and Politics in the Third World.* She was working at a regular bar and taking cinema classes at City College.

"Still dancing?" she asked me.

"Not as much," I said. "You look good."

"Thanks," she said, with a relaxed nod of the head. I noticed she didn't return the compliment and walked off toward the stairs, trying to avoid my reflection in the windows and the February puddles outside.

Life continued to accelerate and career onward. The thing was, I wasn't getting anywhere. While the world around me was in a high-speed spin cycle, I was simply sucked back by the centrifugal force and stuck to the side like a wet shirt, not moving.

It was around this time that I began to have dreams that somebody was going to cut off my hair. I'd get up in a half sleep, walk into the bathroom, clutching my curls in my fist, bind the whole mess in a hair elastic, then return to bed. In my perverse, semi-awake logic, if my hair was "together" in a ponytail, it would not be hacked off by my nebulous predator. I was only vulnerable when it was loose. I found myself waking in shock, grabbing my head, bunching my hair in my hands, grasping it in a big ball to make sure it was still there. And then I began to sleep in my wigs.

I had sex. I put my money away. I wrote lies to my dad in Karachi, and called him on the phone and lied to him across the miles for fifty cents a minute. There were a lot of men during that time. And there was a lot of money. And there were a great many lies.

Nobody stayed. I woke up alone and tired on Valentine's Day and sleepily drank water from a vase of flowers beside my bed. Roses from Marty. Still fresh, and there was aspirin in the water. Almost every morning I half electrocuted myself on the toaster. Dad was right about that wiring.

This being late winter, my upstairs neighbor had developed an unbelievably raucous cough to go with his laugh. He gulped and guffawed like a carnival sideshow as I tried to read serious news in the paper.

Each day began in the mute company of expiration dates, daily values, and bar codes. I had become tired even of my cereal boxes. They would, it seemed, have made the perfect vehicle for struggling painters and photographers to show their work to the world each morning. That I would have liked, to wake up to a low-fat, high-fiber abstract oil painting full of pain and meaning. It would have made a welcome change from abducted toddlers, rendered digitally into adolescence in age progression photos, or the daily breakfast time portrait gallery of wholesome cereal box cover models, also rendered digitally into adolescence but from the other direction. They could take their flake-peddling good health elsewhere and I would pick a break-fast food better suited to my new personality. Grapefruit, perhaps. Yellow and green. Soft and bruised. But bitter and thick skinned.

One morning, as I paged through the paper, a small, italicized headline once again caught my eye. "Is sex taking over your life?" It was an ad for a support group for sex addicts. I thought about going, just to prospect for new business. I thought about going anyway, to get my head straightened out. I wanted to see a shrink, but I didn't have health insurance and didn't care to spend the money. If I worked just a few more hours in the smut business, I could almost have saved enough.

Below the advertising was another one that read: "Consider an act of love." It was a call for sperm donors.

My sexuality was all bravado. Sex had become a "procedure" and I didn't feel a thing.

I had nowhere to go but the inside of my head. Nobody wants to hear about somebody else's lovers. They're like dreams. They're only interesting to the person who had them.

I started to wonder whether I was frigid. It was one of those woefully insulting, outmoded medical adjectives, like "melancholy" or "barren." Ever so slightly misogynistic, yet somehow so descriptive. I knew there was probably a more clinical name for it now. Some kind of three-word tag ending in "syndrome" or "disorder" that has since been reduced to a trendy little acronym like SLD or UDS. But "frigid." I almost relished the word. It conjured up a satisfyingly vindictive image of a cool, empty deep freeze. If you could open it up at all, all you would find is a hollow, white void of mist and frosty stuff, harsh and cold and unpleasant to touch.

I began to think about the mythologies of women with which we malnourished young children. The princess so sensitive she could feel a hard, dried-up pea through twenty-seven feather beds and twenty-seven mattresses.

Some nights, and then some mornings, I would talk to myself in a different voice. Like a professional witness or schoolyard snitch, it told me things I wasn't sure if I could believe. It told me I hated having sex with them. Hated touching their skin, hated the way they touched me. I hated the coarse hair on their chests, the gritty surfaces of their back and shoulders. I hated the rough chins against mine. Some of them fucked like rapists, oblivious, desperate. I hated the smell of them. Even out of the shower, even *in* the shower it was dirty. I hated having to look into their bloodshot eyes as they came, like drunks on the verge of throwing up. I faked every aspect of my pleasure. I think I thought it would get better. Sometimes I left this world altogether, or was half asleep. Or I lay patiently through it, waiting for it to be over, like a trip to the dentist. I told them it was good, like they wanted to hear. And I told them I loved them. But I didn't.

And sometimes, in the middle of the night, I'd wonder about those wives and daughters and bachelor party fiancées. They could be anyone, my friends, somebody like my mother, somebody like me, disrespected and lied to and betrayed. I wanted to befriend and console them. I wanted to start a book club with them and make them tea.

One night, the phone rang at 2 A.M. I thought it was the smoke alarm, at first. Phones always seem louder at that hour.

"Dad?"

"Dad? *Dad?* It's *me.*"

"Oh," I croaked, "Hi . . ."

"I need you. I'm sorry. You're the only person I can call."

"All right."

"Can you come over. *Please.* I'll never ask you again."

"OK. Where are you?"

"At home. Get in a cab. I'll pay you back. Just get here as fast as you can. You're the only person I can reach."

The voice was tearful, tired and shredded. Breathless and weak.

"I'll come," I said. "Where are you?"

"At—you don't fucking know who this is, do you?" heaved the voice.

"No," I confessed, "I don't."

"It's Mary."

"Mary?"

"Mary. One of the many other people that you fail to notice inhabiting the planet with you."

She stood on the hardwood living room floor, brittle and white. At first it seemed she stood in a bed of rose petals, or red and white confetti sticking to her bare feet. But the leaves did not flutter about beneath us as she breathed. The red was blood and the white bits were the torn-up pages of her address book. The blood had soaked the tiny shreds of paper and glued them to the floor in nasty wet gobs. It was blood that dripped stickily down her blue-white legs from beneath her dress as she stood gasping at me.

With swollen, prizefighting eyes Mary slowly focused on me as I crossed the room.

"I tore it up," she said, pointing at the mess of A's through L's and M's through Z's. "I tore it apart. Nobody would have come."

She clutched her stomach and collapsed on the sofa, wadding the slack fabric of her Indian print dress into an absorbent ball and stuffing it between her thighs.

"Where's T-Bone?" I asked, rudely.

"T-Bone? *T-Bone?*," she repeated back, as though she still couldn't believe what an incredibly stupid name he had. "T-Bone's long gone. He moved to New Mexico. There was only one left . . ." She picked a business card off the coffee table, and held it up to my face. "I had nobody else, Juliet. I had no choice."

I stared quizzically at the card. " Martin L. Fisher. Director of Client Marketing and Integrated Sales?"

She almost laughed, and turned it over. My name and number, which she'd scrawled on the back of that business card all those months ago in the poor light of a street lamp and neon sign. We never did go out dancing.

"So I think I'm having a miscarriage," she said to me quite politely. "Can you take me to the hospital?"

"How far along are you?" I asked, stupidly, as though inquiring into her progress on a crossword puzzle.

"I don't really know. A couple of hours."

"That's not what I meant. Whose is it?" Whose *was* it?"

"What? What are you talking about? Mine. Whose does it look like?"

We held hands. She slept and shifted on a high, firm hospital bed as a television blinked silently in the corner, stuck up on the wall like a TV in a bar. She ate corn flakes and cried a little and I brought her some bubblegum magazines filled with pictures of puffy-lipped, golden-skinned teens in lip gloss and tiny shorts. They only let her stay a day or two, but it was enough time for us to talk.

"I would have had it," she confided, dipping a ball of cottony dough into the thick green pea soup.

"Maybe it's a blessing in disguise," I said.

"Maybe," said Mary, "Children can be sort of messy . . ."

I think at that moment we both thought of her living room floor sticky with paper and cigarette ash and tears and blood. We both had a little laugh.

"I've had enough," she said.

"Finish it," I urged, looking into the bowl.

"Not that. I'm getting out of the business."

"Nursing?"

"*Nursing?*" Mary shrieked in that way of hers, that way she had of repeating words or phrases with a cruel and incredulous emphasis, just to highlight the stupidity of the question.

"I thought that's what you were doing these days," I said, quietly.

"Nursing? Well, you could call it that." She coughed out a raunchy laugh.

"You never answered me properly about the baby," I said, rather meanly. "Who was the dad?"

"Don't know. Any one of about seven people."

"Seven. That's not too bad."

She looked up to the television for a moment. A Forbes 500 software executive was crying at us in a sharp suit, pointing into the camera, his muted pleas reaching out toward us at weak levels from the low-volume TV up there on the wall.

"Just bring my daughter back safely. We know she's alive. We just want her back." Then they cut to a smiley yearbook photo of the girl with the eyebrows.

I thought for a minute that Mary was starting to cry, although maybe it was just an awkward mouthful of soup passing hotly down her throat. She bit her top lip like a little kid.

"The world's so sad anyway. What's the point of dragging someone else through it with you?"

She glanced into her bowl and fished out a tiny pink cube.

"Christ," she sighed, rubbing her eyes. " Why'd they have to give me the soup with the little pieces of dead flesh floating around in it? I asked for the vegetarian menu."

They let her go home the following day. After this Mary disappeared. She quit the club, her phone was disconnected, and when I stopped by her house a few weeks later, I found it had been rented out to a young Asian couple and their small daughter. The child opened the door when I rang the bell. She was one of the most beautiful little girls I think I'd ever seen, with light brown, eggshell skin, dark hair so shiny it looked like it had been polished like fine wood. She said a single word to me in another language, before her father stepped up behind her in the doorway, a young man in a suit, holding a pair of glasses in one hand and a cup of chocolate pudding in the other.

"Sorry," I said, eyes down, "I was looking for somebody else."

"I am somebody else," said the man, though I'd been talking to the girl, not him.

When I did hear from Mary again, she was in another world. But that wasn't for a long time.

For a while, I looked for Mary in the newspaper, wondering if she'd reemerge, and I tried to guess which section: local news, arts, politics . . . obituaries. Instead I learned that a lot full of sport utility vehicles had been set alight in an arson attack in Reno, Nevada, and that police suspected a radical environmentalist organization. I learned that the East Bay teenager was still missing and hopes were fading. I learned, on my twenty-third birthday, April 3, 1996, that they'd arrested the Unabomber. He was a lonely and paranoid former math professor who lived in small cabin in Montana, in desperate need of an editor, a brisk shower and shave, and a good haircut. I learned that Marty Le Beau wanted to sell his building and was evicting all his tenants, who, in turn, had called for a boycott of an exhibit of experimental sculpture at the gallery bearing his name, even though the artist was an impoverished grant recipient and this was her first real show. Another of life's disgusting messes in which I felt unaccountably complicit.

Alone at home, sinking into my beanbag, I came close to calling Marty, but I decided there and then to stop seeing him. Evicting his tenants... what an asshole. Instead I rifled through my Cherry Tree matchbook and business card scraps for new business. In my purse I found half a movie ticket for *The People vs. Larry Flynt.* I'd been trawling for phone numbers a while back and, after some agitation from me, a good-looking young man had scribbled something on the back of this ticket and thrust it rather aggressively down my stocking top.

"There you go, if that's what you want," I remember him saying. "Make sure you call it."

Uncovering the number again now, I rolled over on my side, reached lazily for the phone, dialed, and prepared myself for a breathy hello. Seconds later, I found my finger pressed painfully into the hang-up button, exhaling hotly into my folded up knees, unable to raise my head.

It was the telephone number of a mental institution.

Pink Shots

I decided to take a break from personalities after that. It was all becoming too caustic and demoralizing. I would try professional porn, instead. That way, when the photographer said cut, I could stop what I was doing and go back to being myself.

It was pretty easy. Like most things, just a phone number away. Good old *Bay Guardian,* its back pages reliably filled with all kinds of phone numbers that could get you into all manner of dicey situations. Bars and hotels, escort referral services, S & M clubs, massage parlors, wild side adventures of every stripe and color. Then an equal quantity of corresponding numbers so that you could get yourself out again. Sex addicts anonymous, AA, HIV testing, yoga retreats, detox.

I started out on the tame side. His name was Roy Fox and he had a proper photographer's studio in Emeryville. We arranged a date and he picked me up at the MacArthur BART station in a white minivan one free afternoon. He was much younger and rather different from the image of him I'd formed based on his rather suave and business-like phone message.

"If you are concerned about maintaining anonymity this is NOT the gig for you." Sure, I was concerned, but nobody looked at porn.

I'd pictured Roy as a fiftyish, short, balding man whose little hair would be gray. As it happened, he was almost fifty, but looked a lot younger. He turned out to be quite pleasant. When he wasn't photographing pussies he did commercial photography.

"But nature photography," he said to me in the car, "nature photography is my first love. Unfortunately I don't have the time for it that I'd like. You know how it is? Porn isn't all mafiosos and guys with cigars and gold chains. A lot of us are just nice folk subsidizing our real interests. Our true passions. Is that true of you? This probably isn't your full-time career pursuit either, is it? Or is it?"

Or was it? True passions? I made a mental note to reestablish what those might be as we pulled up in a quiet, industrial section of the East Bay.

He seemed to have brought me to an abandoned warehouse, about as far from nice folk as you could get, short of the bottom of the bay.

"You're not going to kill me and dump my body, are you?" I asked as we got out of the car.

"Ah," Roy laughed. "You see, when I said I wanted to shoot you . . ."

In fact, inside the studio, he had a large, professional setup. One corner of the warehouse was "dressed up" as a cheesy bedroom, with a desk, fluffy carpet, corny hotel-room-style oil painting of prancing horses, and a double bed with pink satin covers.

I followed as he led me to his office. Passing through a small hallway, we walked by a horrible scaffold, hung with whips, gags, and a balaclava helmet. Roy hastily pulled a sheet over it.

"Sorry," he said. "I do the occasional bondage shoot. Must remember to put that thing away. I did a commercial job for Longs Drugs in here the other day. Product shots and so forth. You should have seen the stylist's face when she saw that."

Sitting in the office, which doubled as a dressing room, I completed a questionnaire about what I would and wouldn't do. It was divided into various categories, each category split into "Soft Core," meaning "faking it" and "Hard Core," meaning I'd actually be willing to do it.

I checked just about everything except anal sex, but included an asterisk indicating that I "might try unchecked items in future."

Roy showed me some pictures he'd had published in *Eager Beaver* and *Tail* magazines, and some black-and-white glamour shots taken to advertise an escort named Kara, who had ludicrously huge fake breasts.

"Those look terrible," I said. "I wonder how much she paid for them?"

"We did them on trade," said Roy, "They're a little contrasty, but I'd rather have that than grain."

Roy, it turned out, was quite a serious aesthete. He gave me a hard time about the fluff on my upper lip and didn't like any of the outfits I'd brought. Instead he loaned me one from his "wardrobe." White stilettoes a size too big, into which the last model had stuffed toilet tissue, and a silly, pink, two-piece neglige that kept coming undone.

"Wow," he said, before we started, "I just want to tell you, you have a beautiful, amazing body."

I decided he said this just to jack up my confidence.

"Bet you say that to everyone," I said. "Maybe you're used to shooting fatter women for your big girl Web site. Do you say that to them, too?"

"Well," said Roy with some thought, "to the bigger girls, I usually rephrase it a little. I say, 'Oh boy, *they're* going to *love* you.'"

"Guys prefer plump women, don't they? Not that I care."

"Sure. Some. To be honest, you could stand to gain a few pounds. You'd look much better naked with a bit more meat on your bones. I feel like I've dressed up a concentration camp corpse."

We did a brief shoot of stills and video, with all kinds of elaborate lighting. I was incredibly white, and Roy did me the special favor of using a special filter on the lens to give me a simulated tan.

I played with dildos and acted out horribly fake orgasms. I learned the two staple looks of the pornographic still: "ooh" (eyes half closed, lips half closed as though blowing out candles on your birthday cake) and "ahh" (eyes fully closed, mouth open). That part was fairly easy. The hardest thing was to smile. This was supposed to be sex, I thought. Why would I be smiling? The most absurd thing he had me do was to put the vibrator in my mouth and suck on it. It tasted of rubbing alcohol, and I started making faces.

"What's the problem?" asked Roy.

"Sorry," I said. "This scenario doesn't make sense to me. Nobody does this! It's cold. The girl's not enjoying it, the dildo's certainly not getting off on it . . ."

"The readers will, though."

"Ah readers," I said. "*Readers.* Forgot about them."

At one point, as I lay on the bed with my legs apart while he moved in for some close-ups, Roy stopped looking through the lens for a minute, stood up, and stopped the proceedings entirely.

"Er, Juliet," he said, "could you do me a favor and take the price tags off the bottom of your shoes?"

I sat up and looked at the soles. "50% off. $11.50." Roy

brought over the ubiquitous rubbing alcohol and I scraped away at the sticky, orange label.

"We don't want you looking *that* cheap," he said.

Roy was, to his credit, more enthusiastic about the technical aspects of photography and video than he was about cheeseball sex. He explained all about white balance and diffusion. I learned what a "pink shot" meant. Sort of like the old money shot when no boys are around.

I only made $175 that day. Not much, really, but I could have worked in an office all day for that. This only took a couple of hours and then I returned to the city and went to a free photography exhibit on the theme of summer and winter in various states. Roy had some pictures in it and had given me a couple of free passes. It was beautiful. New York and Alaska offered quite a contrast.

My next shoot was with a guy from Los Angeles, putting together a girl-on-girl series. Crazy Chris, he called himself. After failing to coax me to fly down south to drink champagne in his Hollywood hot tub, he flew up to San Francisco and booked a room at a five star hotel on Union Square. He'd lined up a couple of other models to shoot with, a pair of lap dancers who lived in Oakland, one Spanish, one Brazilian.

Chris was young, sweet, and, again, quite professional. He

was tall and muscular with a shaved head. He reminded me of Mr. Clean from the household detergent of the same name.

He worked on his laptop, checking e-mail while I took a shower and drank a five-dollar bottle of lime mineral water from the mini bar. As I was drying off, he put his head around the door and asked, "How are you down there? Well manicured?"

"I'm pretty hairy, actually," I said. "I'm not shaved or anything."

"Would you mind?" he asked.

So I stepped, shivering, back into the tub and Chris handed me a brutally sharp razor and a small bar of hotel soap.

"Are you sure?" I whimpered. "This is going to take about three hours."

I begin hacking and scraping my genital area until dark pink streaks began to seep into the creamy puff of soap suds. Chris finished me off with his battery-operated beard trimmer, turning me over onto my knees and mowing me with a swift buzz and tickle between the cheeks.

I rinsed and patted myself gently, smearing the precious ivory fluff of the hotel towels with blood and hair.

"Ow," I said, emerging from the bathroom, covering myself between the legs. "I don't think that was a very good idea."

And when Nuria and Sabrina arrived they took one look and said, "No. Absolutely no. We have good bikini wax already."

I tried to keep my pelvis pointed to the floor as we faked a three-girl orgy while Crazy Chris followed us around with his video camera.

When it was done, Chris gave us each our three hundred dollars and then he called room service and ordered about two thirds of the menu—pasta, salad, fish, steaks, wine, beer, crème brûlée and apple pie. We three girls hid under the bedsheets giggling naked as the food was delivered and a table set up. Then we ate in the nude and watched a movie on cable. *The Muppets Take Manhattan.* It was actually quite funny.

I didn't like being bald at all. What it exposed was just a little too much information. But afraid of that itchy, stubbly middle ground, I stayed shaved for a few weeks, the rash and razor burn slowly improving until I was as smooth as a preadolescent girl. I hadn't seen it like that since I was twelve. It was all a rather sad, simulated time warp that eventually became much too perverted and unsettling after a couple of shifts at The Cherry Tree. I took a week off and grew a little hair back. It took a month to fully cover me again, the new tendrils creeping through punk pussy and awkward new wave phases before settling softly back into fully fledged hippy hair.

The Mr. Clean shoot had gone so well, I became rather cavalier after that. The Brazilian girl had given me the number of a British guy called Monty who shot bondage. I called him up.

"Brilliant, brilliant. I'm always looking for new models," he explained in a thick Liverpool accent. "I've worked with a couple of birds from The Cherry Tree before. They're always fab." I felt like I was talking to one of the Beatles or something. I thought briefly about my late mother. Not a good time for that.

"Now, what are your limitations?" he asked.

"Um . . . Well, I wouldn't put on a Nazi uniform or anything like that."

"I should think not! But do you consider yourself a dom or a sub?"

"What?"

Unaware of what he meant, my thoughts turned vaguely to cheap snacks.

"Do you usually dominate, or are you more the submissive type?"

"Submissive? Definitely not submissive. Not very domineering, either," I said.

"Sounds like your not really a scene person," Monty went on. "That's fine. At least half the girls I work with are just models."

"Right," I said slowly. "Not really into it as a lifestyle thing."

"So, you're pretty vanilla in your own sex life, then, are you?"

Until working with Monty, I wouldn't have quite put it that way, but as it turned out I was vanilla diluted. I was cream cracker. I was stale white bread. I was boiled potato, *Reader's Digest,* and PBS.

We shot in a dungeon. Not actually in the basement of some Gothic mansion, but in an unmarked warehouse building across from a lumber company on Bayshore Boulevard. Public transport went nowhere near it, so I picked up a cab from outside one of the hotels downtown, which I figured would be slightly cheaper than taking one all the way from my place.

"Four seventy-five Bayshore Boulevard," I said.

"What, the airport?" asked the driver.

"Just 475 Bayshore. That's all I know," I replied. Don't ask. Don't ask. Don't ask.

The driver nodded. "What you doing there? Where you going? Is for what?"

"Helping my friend shoot a video."

I was the first to arrive, and I sat on a couch in the reception area reading *Skin Two* magazine. Soon after, Monty showed up with a video cameraman and a woman with a stills camera. I liked Monty at first. He was youngish with a well-fed, schoolboyish demeanor. He opened up our room, a carpeted, red-walled space filled with a padded table, a cage, a scaffold, and an unsavory assortment of chains, whips, and paddles. One wall reminded me of a saddle room, hung with ropes and straps, bits and bridles, like a stable I'd visited once when I went pony riding as a child in Santa Cruz.

I lay on the table and we started with a basic "hogtied"—hands and feet bound behind my back—and moved on from there, as the videotape rolled and the camera clicked.

The ropes were soft, and I was limber from dancing, so I could get into all kinds of contorted positions, which Monty fully exploited. He wore a full mask, like an executioner, whenever he came into the frame to lash my poor buttocks with his whip—which I thought was rather cowardly and not very egalitarian at all. Still, looking for equanimity in a domination video was rather like looking for toilet paper on a water sports shoot.

Most of what happened on that shoot belongs exclusively in the naïveté department. At first, I liked being tied up. I actually found it relaxing. Totally bound, I was absolved of all responsibility to *do* anything. For a person so used to moving and generally being physical for the entertainment of others, it was all quite liberating. Action, on my part, was eliminated. I had no choice, there was nothing I could do so nothing could be required of me, and somehow that set my mind free. I could have dozed off in some of those positions. At first.

The mousetraps on the nipples were painless, the clothespins on the genitals, also fine. But, the spanking genuinely hurt. We'd established a safe word, "Yellow," which I was supposed to say when I really wanted to cut, but once I was gagged by a red, rubber ball, held between my teeth with a strap-on muzzle, I couldn't pronounce a single consonant.

Yet every time Monty ungagged and untied me to start the next setup, he asked me if I was OK, as though we had simply stopped sharply at a traffic light in his car, and every time I would smile and say yes.

"Doesn't this turn you on at all?" puffed Monty, wrenching my arms above my head and securing them to the top of a metal scaffold.

"Not exactly," I said. "Don't you worry that this promotes violence against women?"

"Not really," Monty went on cheerfully, placing shackles around my ankles, "It's not gender specific. There are just as many magazines and sites of men being flogged by women. The genre's quite democratic in that respect."

Halfway through the shoot, as the tears began to well up in my eyes, I decided I was a dom, after all. I would have given all the money back just to have wrenched that whip from his hands, tied Monty down, and beaten him within an inch of passing out. Either that or turned him over to Amnesty International, the bastard.

As I kneeled on a Plexiglas table, hands tied to a pole above my head, knees apart and tethered, I turned to Monty and asked, "So, this is your main gig, is it? Does your family know what you do for a living?"

"Oh yes!" he said. "And my father's a priest, as well. A Jesuit priest."

Before I could respond, he'd slipped the gag on again. I felt somehow safer after that comment about his dad. As though God were watching out for us. God, the quintessential sado-masochist, if ever there was one. God, a closet bondage freak. But even God, watching *that*? Surely not.

"How are you, sweety? All right?"

"OK, I guess," I said.

"That's it for today. Cup of tea?" Monty asked, releasing me at last.

"Thanks."

"Oh dear," he said, looking at my backside with mild concern. "You're a bit red on the bottom."

I looked down at my buttocks to find them covered with tiny purple and red dots They weren't even proper, cool-looking bruises. He'd broken all the blood vessels under my skin, so that I was left with a mess of ugly, inky freckles that looked like varicose veins.

"Never mind," said Monty, handing me a cup of Earl Grey. "Next time you should mention that spanking is one of your limitations." Next time. As if there would be a next time after that.

I had to wear a silly little ballerina skirt at The Cherry Tree for a whole week. Oddly enough, that same week, I noticed that one of the other dancers, a new girl from L.A., also took to the stage with a giant, blue bruise on her buttock. It was about four inches in diameter, as dark as a tattoo, and much more dramatic looking than my stippling, like she'd been hit by a paddle. She made no attempt to hide it, but appeared instead to be showing it off to the clientele as some kind of fetish extra. I never asked her about it, but at one point I silently lifted my floaty white tutu and showed her mine. She winked at me and whispered, "Naughty girl." I felt better after that, like there was some kind of solidarity among the spanked.

The next ad I answered called for lusty girls for sex videos. Instant Cash! Amateurs welcome. Impatient as always, I was at once sold on the whole "instant" concept. Always had been. Cameras, mashed potatoes, cash. Couldn't wait.

The man who had placed the ad was a middle-aged architect called Eddy, a semi-retired Texan with a plush flat and a hot tub at the top of Russian Hill. I met him for coffee at the Ground Hog Cafe. He was tubby, with thinning hair, and looked as though he belonged playing the jovial next door neighbor on some 1970s sitcom. He had that kind of eye-rolling, underdog cheeriness. As he unfurled stretches of his cinnamon roll and dipped them into his coffee, I pictured him wrestling with a garden hose on a tungsten-lit sunny day and getting squirted in the eye with water.

"It's safe sex, and I don't show the tapes to anyone," he explained, in a loud, immodulated voice. The young man working on his laptop at the next table looked over his shoulder at us. I scooped my hair up and looked away, trying simultaneously to change my appearance and hide my face.

"They're for my private collection," Eddy went on. I nodded in approval, trying to get him to shut up or keep it down. The man next to us turned back to his keyboard and resumed typing. I wondered whether he was transcribing our conversation.

"Like what I see! Hope you'll give me a try, Juliet! You only regret the things you *don't* do, after all!"

We made a date for a Tuesday evening.

He played CDs of the Pet Shop Boys and the Kingston Trio and plied me with nice chocolates and a tiny sniff of coke, before tiptoeing stealthily off to his bedroom to fetch his video camera. He returned naked except for his tie and sat the tripod and camera at the foot of his green velvet sofa.

He lay back and I straddled him, my knees sinking into the mossy cushions on either side. I gyrated up and down on top of him for a while, every now and then looking into the lens for dramatic effect. After a few minutes, I had to visit the bathroom, so I slid off him, making a giggly apology.

And as I passed by the video camera, I noticed it didn't appear to have a tape in it. It didn't even seem to be turned on.

I turned toward Eddy and said, "Eddy, baby, I think you forgot to turn your camera on!"

He rolled over onto his elbows, laughed, and nodded.

"It doesn't matter," he said.

"But you won't be able to watch us back," I said.

"I don't actually use the camera," he confessed. "It's just a prop."

"But I thought you collected sex videos."

"That's just how I advertise it," he said, cheerfully. "I used to just advertise for girls to come over here and have sex with me, but I didn't get as many takers."

I was silent for several seconds, the word "Oh" written all over my face, but not really coming out.

"I can go get a tape and video us, if you prefer," he said. "Would you like that? It's up to you. You'll get your money whether I tape us or not."

Oh. I thought. Oh. Great big fucking oh.

A few weeks later, Roy Fox called to see if I wanted to visit his studio and look at slides of our shoot. This turned out to be far more sadomasochistic an experience than the bondage session. I sat at a table with a loupe, gazing at shot after shot of my hairy, raw genitalia. I looked old and used up. Not like the creamy-skinned, doe-eyed sex kitten I'd envisioned at all. I had dark circles under my eyes and brownish shadows between my legs. My arms appeared thin and sinewy like a marathon runner's, my breasts small and insignificant.

"What do you think?" Roy asked, "I'd be happy to make you some prints for your portfolio."

I thanked him and said I'd call, but I never did. The fact was, I couldn't handle looking between my own legs at all. I never modeled again after that.

A few weeks later, Roy left a message and told me he'd sold

some of the pictures for *Over 40* magazine. Over 40! I was only twenty-three.

I never saw them in print. Sometimes, when I was shopping for soap and sodas at Ng's, I would glance up to the top shelf of his magazine rack and wonder. Once I did reach up and leaf through. I didn't see myself, but there was a photo, in a magazine called *Foxy Fifty,* of a voluptuous brunette, spread-eagle on that bed of Roy's. I recognized the picture of the horses on the wall in the background, and she was wearing the same pink lingerie he'd loaned to me.

It was too early for my photos. The print magazines worked several months ahead. Still, as time went on, I thought about the commitment I'd made in doing those pictures, the fact that no matter where I went now, no matter what I did in the future, they'd always be out there. I wondered if anybody I knew would ever see me, legs spread, trying to smile, sucking on a rubber penis. But to this day, nobody has ever said anything, so I assume nobody ever did.

Unknown Host

There were third-to-last straws, second-to-last straws, and final straws, and I tested my strength for a long time to see how many I could sling over my back before they eventually broke me.

Oddly enough, my first-ever client came back to me. The old, bearded guy who'd taken me at the Days Inn. He asked for me at The Cherry Tree and we sat together, he sipping his cognac and I flirting with the edge of a martini glass, but closing my lips around the cold rim before a drop of that poison touched so much as my two front teeth.

"What's your name?" I asked, officiously. I no longer sat next to them. I sat opposite them now, as though conducting an interview. Insurance claims, lost luggage.

"David S—Slattery," he answered.

"So David S—Slattery, what's your real name?"

"Actually David Slater's my real name. But I go by David Slaughter."

"David *Slaughter?*"

Suddenly I wished Mary were still around. Just to hear her repeat it back to me in an incredulous crescendo. "David Slaughter??" David *Slaughter? Slaughter?*" I really missed her sometimes.

He puts his finger to his lip as though his wife were at the next table.

"Should I know that name?" I asked.

"Probably not," he said with a laugh. "You still seem too nice a girl, Julianne."

"Juliet. Not really. A good girl, that is. I never did take your advice."

"What advice was that?"

"About not giving strange men my number."

"That's not what I said," he said with the sharpness of that geometry teacher of whom he so much reminded me. "I said not to tell strange men where you live."

"You're right," I said, nodding slowly. "You did."

"And did you?"

"Well, my dad knows where I live. He's pretty strange."

"And so, Juliet, what's your real name?"

"Juliet is my real name. I think aliases are a symptom of cowardice."

I began to visit him in a secluded room he rented in North

Beach, in a residential hotel called Casa Miranda, across from a small park. There was one narrow door for the whole building. No lobby to speak of. You went straight from the street to the elevator. On the inside of the elevator somebody had stuck a handwritten sign in Italian. I wondered, on my visits, what it said. Solicitors forbidden? No women callers after 10 P.M.? Wipe your feet? Know Thyself?

The hallway to his single apartment was soft with a golden lentil carpet that took the edge off our footsteps, kept our secret. Slaughter was always hushing me, looking over his shoulder. He'd draw the shades and the white lace curtains as soon as we entered the room. He'd wash his hands in the corner sink, before opening a warm bottle of lager that he pulled from the stash in the bottom of the closet. He liked fancy Cognac, and he'd drink that, too, then start rubbing his bearded face across my cheeks. Everything about him was rough, and his bristles and whiskers left me feeling as if the surface of my skin had been swept with a coarse broom.

Slaughter liked to play. He dressed me up in cowboy hats and hippy T-shirts and took Polaroid photos of me standing stupidly on the lilac bedspread, slowly sinking into the single bed as the pale web of drapes fluttered back and forth in the breeze toward my thighs, as though some purer, prettier force were trying to dress me for Holy Communion, reaching out to cover me up.

He had a good collection of porn, and sometimes he'd push

a tape into the mouth of the VCR and watch hot, ugly video while I lay on the bed, looking at the cracks in the ceiling. I began to make paths and maps again, but now the lines in the shabby paint and plaster seemed only to remind me of a network of human veins, the arteries of a body so thin and ill it had become translucent, revealing a sorry maze of channels and vessels, unable to deliver the correct fluids or a strong enough mix of life.

When he was done, he'd pop the tape out and suddenly the panting, moaning blonde instantly gave way to a news anchor, reporting a drop in interest rates or a rocky ride on the NASDAQ. Sometimes Slaughter would amuse himself with a little game, in which he'd deliberately keep punching the switch between TV and tape, so that the nightly business reports were cut together with a hot-tub three-way or the thrusts and screams of girl-on-girl cunnilingus. The network newsbodies would chirp relentlessly on, with snippets about the Dow Jones, solemn and oblivious, while seemingly all around them, the world was engaged in high-pitched, over-acted feats of pleasure.

Slaughter told me he loved me once, flopped over my back, while I lay idly and passively watching *Celebrity Weddings* on TV. I didn't answer, they cut to a commercial, and I rolled over to face him.

I looked at his seedy eyes and said to him, "You know what I like about TV light? It changes, like the sun." And we sat for a moment, consumer culture flickering across our faces in shades of red and blue.

Slaughter was an ass, but an honest ass. You knew where you stood with Slaughter. He was arrogant, yet oddly insecure, always proclaiming himself a genius loudly in the few bars and restaurants in which he could comfortably hang out.

"Genius. Genius. Why do you keep saying that?" I snapped at him once. "If it were true, I'm sure other people would have spotted it by now."

The fact is, he had a fantastic head for facts and figures, people, places, and events and knew how to form the semblance of an argument by calling upon the hard details of politics and history. But I came to notice that his mind was filled with strange paranoias and fictions and one-sided rants. Incapable of rational argument, he was utterly unable to grasp the concept of diplomacy, of a two-sided debate in which some degree of merit is afforded each party. He was quick and articulate but unreasonable to the point of stupidity, to the point of madness. This extended to everything from to his cultural preferences to sending his food back to the kitchen for no good reason.

"Music is dead. It's been dead for years. Nobody has played music since 1969. What's left is just noise, commerce, tattoos and navels."

"The *New York Times* is a heap of crap. It's the worst newspaper in the Western world. I've seen better journalism in community college newsletters."

"Carter should never have been president. Gerald Ford may have been one of the best presidents we ever had. And I'll tell you why."

"No good can come of NAFTA. Mexico is attached to this country like a piece of dead skin. If it wasn't for geography we'd cut that country off us like a bleeding hangnail."

"You, Juliet, have the great misfortune of being part of the most poorly educated and odious generation this country has ever produced."

Sometimes he'd bring me books and magazines, pointing out articles, reading to me arbitrarily in bed or at the table. He was quite fond of *The New Yorker,* plowing through it every week, then hurtling it into the trash, declaring, "It's a *horrible* magazine. *Nobody* reads *The New Yorker* anymore. Who are these hacks? Still blathering on about the Algonquin like anybody gives a fuck."

David Slaughter was a pompous prick. He was just so wrong, so much of the time. And often he surprised me with his ignorance. He once pulled out an old snapshot of himself, younger and slender with dark glasses, a slim-fitting suit and only a squarish patch of beard.

"You look like Phil Spector," I said.

"Who's Phil Spector," he asked.

"Who's Phil Spector? Who's Phil Spector? Phil Spector was a genius!"

On the other hand, he'd talk for hours about the medical

attributes of certain indigenous plants from Polynesia, or the relationship between Kublai and Genghis Khan and the dawn of the proverbial old boys network in modern society. Over Irish coffees in a quiet corner of North Beach he once went on for a good hour about Sierra Leone's diamond mines and De Beers, and the "evil grip that these types of cartels can maintain in the face of capricious new market forces."

One night, as I licked tiramisu from the back of my spoon in some Italian hole in the wall, he related at length his idea for a giant, futuristic novel he wanted to start.

"I'm calling it *Blue Marsupial,*" he said, as he dipped the gray of his mustache into the rich, red tincture of an expensive port. "It'll be a humanitarian investigation into the ethics and commerce of human cloning, set in the year 2050. The subtext is sort of an indictment of the inextricable way in which finance, law, medicine, and the pharmaceutical industry will shape society and business in the first half of the new century. I've essentially constructed a narrative concerning the competing biotech researchers, the politics of the Nobel Prize selection process, and the corrupt, market-driven inner workings of the FDA."

Then he called over to the waiter, told him the port was too sweet and just to bring him a coffee, in a glass, not a cup, and no sugar anywhere on the table, not even on the side.

I shivered as we left the restaurant that night. I was always cold, and Slaughter offered me his coat.

"No!" I begged, wriggling off to the other side of the side-walk. "No, really. Don't. I'd rather be cold." There was something unsettling about wearing his clothes.

But he took it off his back, a thick, wool overcoat, and threw it over my shoulders anyway. The weight of it caused me to slow down a little, and after only a couple of steps I realized why. A hard, heavy L-shape hit me in the hip with each stride. I pulled the coat off my body and turned to David.

"Jesus Christ!" I screamed at him, "I can't wear this coat. There's a fucking gun in the pocket!"

David sort of laughed and shushed simultaneously.

"It's a cell phone," he said, smiling.

"What are you doing with a gun? I hate guns! I hate them! How could you?"

"I'm sorry," I said, quite seriously now, taking the coat back. "I have to protect myself. Death threats. I've had death threats.

"Death threats? Death threats, plural? More than one?"

"More than one."

I had no idea who he was. But we came to a financial arrangement, and I kept seeing him, and only him. I now worked at the club only three nights a week.

Mac was on to me by this time, but the regulars liked me so he kept me on with a click and a cluck and a hard, oblique stare from the corner of his eyes.

Slaughter liked to play in a manner akin to his name. He'd tie me up and get me in trouble for showing up to work with bite marks all over my back.

"I suffer from Satyriasis," he'd say. "Do you know what that is?

"The chronic desire to satirize everything?"

"Male nymphomania." He really was quite disgusting sometimes.

And then one day, as we sat fully clothed in the Casa, watching the Weather Channel one foggy evening in July, everything changed. It seemed we could consort on some kind of friendly intellectual level, like family or classmates. Slaughter quietly smiled as the weatherman swept his hand across the USA graphic to show us the probable path of an area of high pressure. I looked toward the window. The curtains hung still that night, like a couple of dirty bridal veils. Slaughter flipped channels. Bob Newhart reruns, the news, an advertisement for a four-door luxury car, a ghostly and quiet vehicle, with the usual soulless, metallic veneer.

Then a rock documentary about Cat Stevens appeared on one of the music stations. The song "Wild World" was playing and Slaughter said, "This song makes me think of you."

I threw a cushion at him, hard. It skidded past him onto the arm of his chair, knocking the remains of his cognac to the floor, where it was quickly absorbed into the yellow fuzz of the carpet.

"'Wild World.' Good god, it's enough to make me vomit."

But as we both fell silent again, I listened to the words, and I guess it was kind of sad.

Later that night, he paid me and I went to try to a find a cab. As I stood on the corner of Columbus and Green, a couple of young women came up me. They were British tourists, probably in their early twenties, each clutching an array of maps and guidebooks—which, based on their sensible, heavy sweatshirts and long pants against the summer chill, they had read quite carefully.

"Excuse me," said one, "are there any dance clubs in this area?"

"We're trying to find some of the nightspots," continued the other. "Have we come to the right place?"

"Mind you," said the first one, "we're just us two by ourselves, so I suppose we're looking for somewhere where we can have a bit of fun and won't get hassled."

"We were down the road a bit," continued her friend. "But it seemed to be all strip clubs and clip joints, didn't it?"

"I'm sorry," I replied. "I'm just visiting myself."

The girls seemed to be headed in the same direction I was, and I crossed the street to avoid them, then doubled back on myself, walked a block in the direction from which I'd come, and wound up right back outside Casa Miranda.

As I stood stupidly outside, an old man came out. Thinking I was going in, he held the door open for me. Then, as I reentered the tiny foyer, the elevator opened, a couple of guys stepped out, and for appearance's sake I dipped in through the closing doors. I stood for a while, not hitting buttons, waiting until the Casa residents had exited and made their way down the street so that I could step out again and be on my way. But somebody above me called the elevator and I found myself ascending again to the third floor. The doors opened, a woman got in, so I got out.

I walked down the hall and knocked on David's door.

He opened it, still alone with his television and his single bed, no fuss, no surprise.

"Did you forget something?"

"Yes," I said, and then stood dumb, waiting for my line.

"Did you leave something behind?" came the prompt again.

"No," I went on. But I wanted to.

I reached with difficulty into the tight denim envelop of my front pocket and gave him his money back.

"What's the matter?" David asked. "Something wrong with it?"

"It doesn't feel right," I said.

"Well of course not," he said. "Your pants are too tight. You should keep it in your purse."

I stared at him without a word, assuming from the dampened laugh track behind us that he had switched back to *Bob Newhart* after I'd left.

"All right," he said, and he took the money back.

I walked home, stopping off at the supermarket for hot chocolate, cheap shampoo, and bread. When I arrived, I found that somebody had fused all the lights and the power was out in our building. I lit a candle and lay on the floor in half darkness, staring up toward the ceiling. In the gentle light of the flame, I couldn't really see it. For a moment I imagined it was gone, and there was nothing above me but space or the night sky. I slept well that night with my hair loose and my window open about half an inch.

Early in the summer of 1997, I received a letter. Since I didn't possess a credit card or driver's license or own any property, I had so far been spared the usual flutters of postal garbage that is dumped heartlessly into most households every day. I didn't have a household. Just an address. Occasionally, I'd receive a solicitation from child sponsorship programs and a quarterly pitch from a magazine for adoptive parents. I guess it was a by-product of my brush with the fertility clinic, who seemed to have gotten their donor and recipient mailing lists mixed up.

I considered getting involved in something every now and then. Playing soccer with six-year-olds or reading to blind children on Saturday mornings. One night as I lay in bed, and my conscience battered me as I tried to sleep, I imagined I heard the voice of God speak to me about it. He told me that it was all right not to, but at least I'd thought about it, and that was the important thing. And then he said, quite clearly: "Your work is elsewhere." I don't know when I started to think of God, let alone start hearing his voice. It was a male voice, as well, which was a little disappointing. He probably had a beard, too, come to think of it.

I imagined a lot. Lied to myself. I hoped for things. Of course, that voice-of-God thing was just was an excuse, coupled with the fact that I felt I would never have passed the background check. In the future, I discovered I was wrong about this, as I was about so many other things. But I was only twenty-four. At that time, a significant number of twenty-four-year-olds were puffing their chests out and blowing it out of the nostrils as self-appointed sales managers, presidents, and CEOs at dot-com companies. But in four years many of them would be jobless and bankrupt. I may have said and done some dumb things in that era, but I was glad I never got into that racket.

Anyway, I received this personal letter in a plain white envelope. There was no return address, just the handwriting, fat and round in neat, blue ballpoint. Perhaps familiar, perhaps not, difficult to identify or authenticate, like God's voice, I suppose. I tore at the envelope and read.

> *Dear Juliet,*
> *I'm alive! I'm healthy, I'm happy and I feel like I've*
> *come home after years of knocking on the wrong doors.*
> *I am in the Santa Cruz mountains, and I have*

connected with a group of people who have changed my life. Together they encourage and manifest a kindness and generosity of spirit that I didn't believe existed.

We're a family. I know that we used to feel that way at The Cherry Tree. But there was such a sadness and sleaziness attached to it all. We were pandering to a series of images and a fraudulent legacy about our bodies invented by men. I can hardly believe now that I went on for so long peddling my sexuality, the most private and spiritual manifestation of my energy, as a commodity available to the highest bidder. Not even the highest. Any bidder. Sometimes I think I wanted to have that baby just to get them off me for a few months.

When you get paid to work it as long and hard as we did, and you become aware of the dollar value that men will assign to that, you delude yourself into thinking that you are in a position of power. I'm not so sure any more.

I'm living in a large house owned by a man named Stephen. He doesn't go around in robes and own ten BMWs. I firmly believe he's a good soul. There are only adults here—Stephen believes that people should join or leave his house of their own free will, and that this is not the place for children to be sheltered or indoctrinated.

We are self sufficient, each of us working on the small farm where we grow much of our own food. People come and go of their own accord. I think I may stay a while.

For the first time in my life, I wake up with the sun and am truly excited about each day. I used to despise the sunrise, in the city, when I'd been awake all night. It signified the bitter end of something. The dawn of nothing. A reminder that when most of the world was about to start something new, I was burnt up and stamped out and collapsed, only to be prodded and mocked by light and the sarcastic chirp of morning birds.

I'm writing to invite you here, if you should ever need a place to go. We don't have a telephone, so write to me if you decide to come.

By the way, did you see they caught the Unabomber? What a nut job!

With love,

Mary

Mary, if her newfound vernacular was anything to go by, seemed to me to have gotten herself mixed up in some kind of live-in, twelve-step, New Age fiction workshop.

Beneath her name was the return address. A post office box in Ben Lomand, a small town near Santa Cruz. I looked at the loops and swirls of the letter. The last time I'd seen the handwriting it had been in the tatters and fragments of phone numbers and zip codes, in bleeding, wet pieces of paper chaos on Mary's living room floor.

I recognized Mary in the curves of her pen, but almost nowhere in the letter could I hear her voice, her raw laugh. I could no longer see her worried, defensive brow, her finely corrugated upper lip, the delicate shrivel of her thin, white, freckly eyelids. Only in the exuberant, spontaneous closing line about the Unabomber was there any suggestion of Mary's usual bite. I couldn't begin to fathom how this journey from bar snack to bean sprouts could possibly have come about. Mary's new light, swiveled unforgivably into my face, had caught me in a sorry and unflattering pose, apparently horrid and dried up, passed out on the floor after the purgatory of the night shift, phone in hand, desperate and impassioned face buried in the dirty shag of the carpet.

I pushed the letter into my purse along with a grab bag of paper scraps and business cards. One day soon I would reach in and pull something out. If my hand fell to the letter, I might read it again, and maybe write back. If it fell elsewhere, perhaps I'd pick up the phone and call someone. Maybe my bag would get stolen. Perhaps I should leave the damn thing on the bus or throw it away. As it turned out, I held its soft, familiar leather close to my hip, which was just as well, because, pretty soon, it was all I would have.

The taxi driver down on the street below my apartment was honking incessantly as I scrambled for my hairbrush and keys.

"Shut up!" came a voice from a window above. "You sound like a frigging herd of demented geese." I think it was my laughing neighbor, who was a fine one to talk.

The fog was particulary obstreperous that evening, hissing and taunting, slapping faces like a schoolyard bully playing with a wet dish towel. Every now and then I would throw some of my ever increasing cash wad at the various city cab companies. I didn't have a favorite. Whichever company answered their line first—and sometimes, especially on Fridays or in the rain, they never did.

Taxi drivers drove like maniacs, which I hated when I walked, and had to leap and dive away from their obnoxious thrusts at every crosswalk. But when I found myself stuck in their rear seats, plopped down, sinking and sliding on their stale, dark upholstery, I would inwardly curse at every languid pedestrian to hurry up and get their slow ass back onto the sidewalk out of the way.

There was only one thing more frightening than being a pedestrian in the face of a rabid cab driver, and that was being the passenger.

"Do you like this music?" a driver asked me on the way home one night, nodding toward the tuneless punches of contemporary sound bursting intermittently from his tape deck.

"Oh, yes," I replied, "This sounds a little like . . . Gershwin."

"Gershwin? George Gershwin?"

"I mean Stravinsky. I mean John Cage"

"John Cage? John Cage?"

"Who is it?" I asked.

"It's me. I wrote this."

A trumpet repeated fifteen syncopated grunts of the same note, followed by the same on strings in an entirely different key, while, counter to this, a theremin whined away in unmusical spirals around them.

"Oh yes," the driver went on, rubbing his hand over the white scrubbing brush of short, sharp hair that sat, isolated, on a shiny planet all its own. "I've got a PhD in music."

I didn't say anything. Looking at the ceramic, global sheen of his head, my mind had wandered off to the subject of clearcutting in Redwood country and deforestation in South America. I thought about the Santa Cruz Mountains for a minute, and how long it had been since I'd smelled wet trees, or the warm, salty skin of the back of my father's neck, riding the bike in the hills on a Sunday afternoon.

"Aren't you going to ask me why I'm driving a cab?" bellowed the driver, plowing happily through a red light in an apparent attempt to cripple a couple of teenage boys exiting a comic shop and crossing on green.

"I was going to ask you why you're driving a cab like you're part of some kind of mobile, city regulated, vigilante death squad," I replied, as the two boys cursed and flipped me off as if I had arbitrarily ordered their execution from the backseat.

"Because," said the man, who I noted as driver number 382, "I'm a white male and I believe in God."

"I see . . ."

"It's the Politically Correct. The PC won't hire you if you're a Christian, white male. I've written four symphonies and an opera, three books on music theory, one on the history of the Indian raga, and a highly acclaimed article on the relationship between mathematics, probability, copyright, and the structure of the Western musical scale. But the PC," he went on , citing their acronym as though it defined a secret society like the KKK or the CIA, "not many people realize it, but the PC have an unbending bias to their recruitment agenda in the land of academia. Did you go to college? Where did you go to college?"

"UC Santa Cruz."

"PC Santa Cruz! They're the worst offenders in the nation."

"My mother was a teacher there."

"Was she white?"

"Yes."

"Was she male?"

"Yes," I said. "She was white and male and a born-again Christian."

We arrive at The Cherry Tree and I battled with the heavy door against the slight incline of the street, struggling to make a clean, painless exit.

I still tipped the guy.

On another occasion, I'd kept a cab blocking the street in the bus lane, justifiably angering the bus driver who began to honk and yell at the taxi. After I landed on the cab's backseat and we plunged ahead, the driver twisted around in his seat, and started to rant.

"Did you hear that bus driver? Did you hear that?"

"I'm sorry," I stammered, "I came down as quickly as I could."

"Last month, when this happened, I got out of my cab, and I said to the bus driver, 'You continue to harass me and I'm coming up there to rip your throat open.' He told me he had a bus load of passengers and that I was blocking the road."

"But he did. You were."

" . . . And he thought I wouldn't do it. I would do it. I would happily leave my taxi in the middle of the street and I would gladly take the army knife out of my glovebox and cut that bastard across the skin of the neck in front of his entire overstuffed tin can of drunks and lowlifes who would rather pay a dollar to stand swinging and flaying across town for two hours than get where they're going."

"You're an ass," I thought. "I should have you arrested." Instead I nodded and clucked and agreed that the bus driver had been all wrong and how rude. When we were done, I thought about not tipping, but changed my mind and gave him three percent, which I hoped was more insulting.

Taxi drivers were like our Cherry Tree customers. Most were pleasant, but a small scoopful were rotten. And, like a few brown strawberries on your morning cereal, the distasteful ones tended to flavor the whole experience.

I heaved the cab door shut and shuddered out of the chilly clutches of the sidewalk.

"Kearny and Broadway, please."

I made eye contact with a pair of dark brown irises in the car mirror. The eyes stayed on mine for an uncomfortable while, as if conducting a thorough analysis of the soul of a girl who would go to Kearny and Broadway at 6:30 P.M. on a nasty Tuesday night.

I rested my head on the back of the seat and played with the tangles at the base of my neck, the solid weave of hair that I never bothered to locate with brush or comb. It stuck, hard and gritty, in the skin between my fingers and nails, like the fabric of an old rug.

"Do you mind if I keep my window open?" asked the driver, as clothing fluttered against my body in the freezing gusts billowing into the car.

"I'm a little cold, to be honest," I said, figuring on fifteen percent if he'd wind it up. I was pretty tip-conscious, having lived off them for better part of the last two years. The glass pane slid to a compliant close and I shivered and nodded with gratitude.

"You don't mind the radio, do you?" he asked, addressing me again through the horizontal peephole of the mirror.

I shook my head. It was only a taxi, not a chauffeured limousine, after all. I was lucky to be able to afford it.

The driver tweaked the volume up a notch. A series of commercials for mattress centers, menswear and car dealers, and then a return to the show. I slumped, daydreamed, and gazed out at bars and cafés and commuters driving home, undoing ties, sitting in outgoing traffic, tapping on steering wheels, some happily to music, others hammering their gridlock frustrations into the mute, useless vinyl of their dashboards.

Blessed for once with a silent driver, I started to listen to the radio. From the flat, boxed-in sharpness of its crackles and pops, I could tell it was an AM station. A call-in talk show.

I lurched suddenly forward in horror, hand over mouth, and pressed my rigid torso closer to the front seat.

"Are you all right back there?" he asked, "He's a little much, I know. I can turn it off if you want."

"No," I said, mouth falling open cartoonishly into the huge, incredulous O vowel. "Turn it up."

The radio spat a single, staccato note of static, then the program rolled out, with sickening clarity.

"Do you vote, sir? What is your name?

"Jeffrey."

"Do you vote, Jeffrey?"

"Of course I vote."

"And would vote for a black candidate in favor of wasting millions of taxpayers' dollars on reparation just because whites kept slaves two hundred years ago?"

"I didn't say that —I—"

"Because people like you shouldn't be allowed to vote, Jeffrey."

"Are you saying black people shouldn't be allowed to vote?"

"You said that, Jeffrey, not me. Who died for this cause? Who were the architects of the abolition of slavery act of 1833? Not the black man. The white man!"

"But if you hadn't kept slaves in the first place—"

"People and groups of people who lobby and attempt to manipulate the vote on the basis of a single emotional issue are a liability and a threat to our democracy. All women vote based on a single issue. Abortion. If we took away their votes, babies would not be murdered and abortion would be a crime, as well it should be. Next caller. Tess from Boulder, Colorado. Tess, you're on the air . . ."

I lowered my head and sunk my teeth into the skin of my knee.

The driver chuckled and glanced once more into the rearview.

"Sorry," he said, with a nonchalant shake of the head. "What can I say? I'm a fan." He wiped the back of his hand across what I imagined was the faint smirk invisible below the narrow frame of the mirror. "He seems to be on a real tear this evening."

"I know that guy," I replied flatly, looking out the window at a neon beer sign to my right. "I recognize his voice."

"You do? He's lucky to get through. This is a popular show. Number one in the afternoons. With men, that is."

"Not the guy calling in. The one doing the show."

"Slaughter? You know Dave Slaughter?"

"Not very well."

"Wow," said the driver. "Well, I feel like I know him myself. I listen to his show every day. This is like having a celebrity in my cab!" The driver seemed genuinely impressed. "So how do you know David Slaughter?"

"It doesn't matter."

"A lot of people think it's an act, you know. All that ranting and raving. I've heard he's a die-hard liberal pulling a con job for the ratings. Is that true?"

"I hope so," I said, rolling down the window to gulp in a bracing lungful of fog.

It crossed my mind that they hadn't caught the Unabomber at all, and I'd apparently been dating him. I glanced at the meter and started to do the math for the tip, shuffling singles, fives, and tens expectantly in my lap, waiting for the bright orange display to tick over into the next denomination of bills. The fare rolled on into double digits and I snapped a twenty flat between my fingers.

We pulled in toward the curb outside the club. The driver looked up at the well-lit, frozen bimbos on the sign above the door.

"This isn't how you know him, is it?" he asked with a grin. "David Slaughter?"

Stepping out into the street, I let the heavy door crash closed and gave my curly hair a short, ambiguous shake.

"That's not his real name," I replied.

"You. My office. Now."

He didn't raise his voice. He didn't have to. I'd never seen Keith Macintosh looking so terrifying. He grasped my wrist the moment I skulked in the door, his face a horrid strawberry shortcake of angry white and red blotches, veins pulsating in his thick, Scottish neck as if his head had been shut off from his lungs by a large rubber band.

I pulled my hand out of his grip, and he turned his back, snapping his fingers with a short, shrill whistle. "Come here. Follow me."

"Don't whistle at me," I said. "I'm not a dog."

"Yes, you are," he said. "Now get in my office."

Big Mac slammed his body into his institutional gray rolling desk chair, and slapped his hands violently onto his desk, palms spaced dramatically apart like he was about to perform a monstrous piano concerto.

I looked everywhere but into his furious eyes. At the strange hanging calendar of "European Ports and Shipyards," at Olympic rings of old coffee and booze on the loose-leaf paper mess that covered the surface of his desk, at the autographed photograph of some third-rate, late-eighties college football player on the wall behind him.

"I received a little," he started, digging his nails beneath flaps of paper, scooping around arbitrarily for something buried.

"A little? A little of what?"

"Don't be stupid. A litter."

"A litter? A litter? What of? Kittens or something?"

"Don't get smart with me, Juliet." He smacked his hand on top of a single piece of stationery, swept it up into my face, then snapped it down in front of him, under his reading light.

"Oh. A letter. A *letter*."

"Yes, Juliet. A litter."

"A letter!" I repeated, melting with the relief that he'd somehow heard from Mary, too, and was concerned or insulted or had come to me for female counsel and enlightenment. "I got one, too," I continued with weak cheer. "I think I know what it says."

"Do you? Do you? Did it say this, Juliet? Perhaps it said this:

"'Dear Club Management:

"'Thanks for a great time at your establishment. Please give a special thanks to the wonderful "Juliet" (probably not her real name) for the wonderful gift that she passed along to me the night of my visit to the City by the Bay. Thanks to you and your thinly disguised (not to say illegal) whorehouse, I now have hepatitis, and so does my wife, Anna, who is three months pregnant.

"'Again, thanks. How about marketing a T-shirt for your clientele: I visited The Cherry Tree and all I found was the pits. You might want to suggest that your employees wear them, too. It might do them good to cover their precious little tits once in a while.'"

He thrust the paper into my hand and I threw it back. The page somersaulted and glided to the floor with inappropriate grace and quiet. It landed facedown.

"Who's it from?" I mumbled, picking gold flakes of polish from my nails.

"Didn't sign it."

"Coward."

"Coward?

"Probably not her real name . . ." I quoted. "Asshole."

"His wife, Juliet? Three months pregnant. Hepa-fucking-titis?" He pushed the edge of his desk, rolled back the chair in histrionic disgust, held his hands in a pastiche of a combined shrug and surrender above his head, backed off, but was still unable to get far enough away from me.

"Hepatitis?" he repeated, "Wake up and smell the shit, love. You broke my rules, you fucking whore. There's families to think about here, Juliet."

"Whose fault is that?" I screamed in return.

"Yours, you stupid little twat. Now get your stuff out of the changing rooms, get out of my club, go home, and don't come back."

He held on to the back of his neck and looked disbelievingly at the ceiling, as if fully surprised the roof hadn't blown off or his head come unattached in the wake of this meteoric outburst.

"All right?" he added, staring right at me.

I had three pairs of boots beneath the dressing room counter, a plastic bag of stockings and thongs and half a tube of body glitter. On my knees, surrounded on both sides by a forest of anonymous, indifferent legs, I dug around for them, next to the trash can, smelling foot odor and the waxy fragrance of makeup and lotion.

I stayed down there, faced with a blur of used tissues and hair balls, watching my tears splat onto the floor, leaving tiny, clean circles in the grime of the linoleum. Everybody looked at me when I stood up, puce and deranged, but nobody said anything. Nobody hugged me, or made me laugh, or asked what was wrong. Nobody told me not to worry, that men were all swine, and come on, let's get a cup of hot chocolate. And it occurred to me that most of the girls around me were new, they were rookies now and strangers. I never talked to them, and barely knew their names. All the old girls had moved on. And for the first time it occurred to me that maybe I really had been there too long.

I let loose my grip on the boot in my left hand, and it dropped back to the floor, its shiny thigh-high tube of black vinyl flopping onto its side and onto the ground like a with-ered beast. There it lay, dead, next to a flimsy bag of flimsy "clothing" and flimsy ideals. I pressed my purse into my hip and left the rest behind. The new kids could fight over my stuff, if they wanted to. I was gone.

I could smell it in the air about ten blocks away. At first it smelled like dirt or exhaust from a seething, overcrowded bus. A thick, noxious odor, it rode along on the wind, entering eyes, nose, and head, pulling me toward it as though this dark invis-ible disaster had been created by a mess of forces especially for me. In fact, I walked toward it because I was walking home, my mind a heavy, hot brick of mixed feelings, cooking and solidifying, not having fully taken form. Though it was dusk, something blacker and nastier than night was closing in, and though the evening was bathed with an unusual late-summer warmth, I became filled with the sense that I was approaching an even greater, surging heat. Walking home that night was like walking headlong into the sun.

My block of Geary Street was cordoned off. There was the finishing tape, and there was a large, sooty-faced man in a helmet telling me to stand back.

"But I just want to go home. I live down there."

"Not anymore, you don't."

Where I no longer lived was a half absence of orange and black, of broken, falling, tumbling, burning chunks of wood, metal, and stone. Smoke churned and spewed from every window of the charred facade, and inside it, behind it, the flames ravaged my little home, and everybody else's, and Ng's corner store, whose windows had melted, whose bottles of cheap rum had blown up like fireworks, whose plastic-covered, out-of-date apple pies and cupcakes had dripped, scalding, into the city floor.

Standing outside with all the others, I thought of my dumb beanbag and started to cry. It was a rare one, an original from the 1970s. It was my mom's. I tried to imagine what kind of stench that orange vinyl would have made as it was eaten by fire, and the rancid fumes of the Styrofoam grains inside it.

The young man next to me put a comforting arm around my shoulder and we stood together as the tired, bruised bodies of the San Francisco Fire Department ineffectively wielded heavy jets of foam into the core of the blaze.

"They think it was an electrical fire," said the man. "Doesn't surprise me. My hair got a new perm every time I flicked a light switch in that place." And he suddenly let out a ridiculous, leaping, gulping laugh that bounced uncontrollable through a range of octaves before its abrupt and awkward death.

I was standing crying in the arms of my laughing upstairs neighbor.

"Is the smoke in your eyes or do you know someone who lived there?" he asked.

"I knew someone," I said. "But it's OK. They got out."

And the tears dried, either scorched out by the heat, or by something else. Like the building, I was gutted, slowly and painfully, as I stood there on the street watching the last of my city life explode and disintegrate in this ravaging, uncontrollable force.

We watched all night, from far away, huddled in blankets, helpless. Everybody cried, no lives were lost, and eventually the whole thing was extinguished, leaving the inevitable, foul heap of foam, water, and sodden, burnt-up crap that we had once called home.

And after the flames subsided, so did my anguish. As the apartment building was violently cleaned out and destroyed, so was I, until it was not loss I felt at all but liberation. It wasn't emptiness I felt. It was an overwhelming sense of space. It was an unfamiliar feeling, but as it flooded me, I knew I'd sensed it once before, the invigorating rush of latitude and possibility.

It was all those years ago, back in Santa Cruz, the day after the earthquake. The day I felt well again and got out of bed to live, free of my illness, or so I thought. What a mess I'd made of things. What an overwrought, far-fetched mess.

I looked down at my feet. I had four jeweled toe rings and gold polish. I ran my hand over the genuine leather of my purse, and I pushed it closer into my outer thigh. At 4 A.M., I would sit in borrowed pajamas at the Salvation Army shelter and go through it.

GREEN

Empire Grade Asylum

Up in the air, cutting arcs in the sky, I could see a tiny, multi-colored neon diamond. It tugged, swooped, and soared again, while down on the beach a man held on tightly to a bright plastic spool, leaning back, arms gently flexing, as though trying to land a great tropical fish as it flapped and struggled to free itself from his line and swim off into the blue. Around his feet and legs his wet dog yelped and leaped upward toward the string. Finally, the string snapped and the object spiraled upward, then nosedived spectacularly into the sand. The dog scrambled over to sniff out the disabled toy, licking at the life-less nylon. Finding it inanimate after all, the dog quickly lost interest and ran off to bark at children.

The man cursed, laughed, then picked up the broken kite. The rainbow fabric had torn off the frame. It flapped around in the breeze, slapping itself on the man's thigh as the wind blew against him.

I don't know why I'd walked toward the beach. Probably because it was the direction that led away from home. I'd left San Francisco on a Greyhound at 6:15 A.M., disembarking at 425 Front Street at 8:55. I was back in Santa Cruz.

"Excuse me," I said to the kite flyer. "Which way is Empire Grade from here?"

The man turned inland. Gesticulating with his free hand, he made a loose semaphore map in the air.

"You'll want to go straight. Northwest on Cliff Street towards First Street. Left onto Second Street and keep going. Hang a right onto Pacific Avenue. Stay straight onto Washington Street. Make a soft right onto Center Street, a left onto Laurel Street. And keep driving for about half a mile. Then another right onto Bay Street. Or is it Bay Drive? I think it turns into Bay Drive. Left onto High Street and you're there. High Street turns into Empire Grade. Just drive on up."

I had stopped listening at Pacific.

"Don't worry, you can ask again," he said.

"That was detailed enough," I replied. "I'll find it."

"I've lived here a long time," he said. "Almost two years, so I know the area pretty well. "I guess you're not from the area?"

"It's been a while." Not worth arguing.

"It's a pretty drive," he said.

I was going to tell him I was walking, but he seemed content with winding his kite string back into a neat, manageable ball, so I left him to it.

The walk took four hours, including aimless wandering and getting lost, asking for directions three more times. Once at a gas station, once at a pet hospital, and finally at a Girl Scout picnic.

Empire Grade twisted up into the Santa Cruz Mountains with a kind of resolute mystery. Not one vehicle stopped to question me or pick me up as I strode endlessly upward. I dropped my head and neck forward, eyes fixed on the tar of the road as it slipped backward and rolled into the balls of my feet with each stride.

I carried over my shoulder a donated army surplus backpack, containing my fabulous leather purse, my wallet, and some outmoded, late-eighties T-shirts. They were gifts from a disaster relief fund, and I loved them in all their unfashionable glory. I loved the matte "Fame" logo on one, and the stupid "Where's the Beef?" slogan on another. I wore a loose pair of men's jeans, held around my waist by a red elastic belt with a snake-shaped clasp. On top, an adopted sweatshirt from the volleyball team of the University of New Hampshire. I was clothed entirely in charitable contributions. It felt good. I hadn't stayed dressed this long in a while.

Empire Grade seemed to wind forth and ascend forever. It wasn't a straightforward road. It was appended with a bewildering number of tangential loops and twists, reaching out toward secluded mountain homes, cul de sacs, and boomerang thoroughfares, forming a curly maze of concealed entrances and exits, several of which I inadvertently wandered down, only to trudge back to the main road, then meander off it again an hour later. Eventually, I became so desperately hypnotized by my own pointless diversions that I came to believe that I would never emerge, but wander in circles forever. I had died, I imagined, and this was heaven. There was no destination anymore. This was all. The journey. The Eastern philosophers were right.

The woman in the front garden was bent over in the sun, pulling weeds from a flower bed beneath the shade of a floppy straw sun hat. She wore a loose cotton dress, so romantically floral that her figure almost merged with the landscape. As I squinted, only her thin, white Q-tip limbs distinguished her from the vegetation. She swayed up and down in a serene rhythm, down to the earth, and back up to her wheelbarrow. She was singing to herself. But it wasn't a soothing Celtic folk song, a hymn or nursery rhyme. She was singing "Ziggy Stardust" with all the wrong words.

"Ziggy played guitar. Jamming good and will it kill him, and the spiders from Mars, he played it left hand, but played it too hard. He was a special man, and they were Ziggy's fans."

Standing by the open gate of the driveway, I laughed loudly.

"It's 'Jamming good with Weird and Gilly,'" I said, "I think."

"What? Who are they?" she said, scrapping her nails into the loose earth, not raising her head.

"They were Ziggy's band. Band. Not fans."

She stood up, pressed her palms into her lower spine, and arched backward, making an enthusiastic stretching noise. She took off her hat, and down spilled the shiny ginger. Finally, we looked at each other.

"Juliet! Fantastic. You look terrible. This is amazing. Come over here. Come in. What happened? You look like hell. You look half dead!"

She dived into me and hugged. Mary was pinkish, healthier now. The crevices and crepes under her eyes and around her lips had all but vanished. Her eyes gleamed as though they'd been lacquered, like the fake eyeballs of a wax museum doll. Her mouth looked red and plump like she'd eaten strawberry sorbet or had just been French-kissed for several hours.

"You look great," I laughed. "Sorry, I don't know what else to say. I haven't talked for a while. To anyone."

I half expected her to back slowly away, and call out a couple of large, mad dogs. Instead she nodded.

"Thanks," she said, "I just took a—" she yawned and stretched again midsentence.

"Took a what? A vitamin? A Valium?"

"A nap."

"About time," I said. And she took my hand and led me up to the house.

Mary called it a group home. I called it a big, fancy rich guy's house. It was a large, three-storied wooden structure, at the top of Empire Grade, down one of those concealed mountain side roads. The outer planks of the building had been painted white. There was parking space for four cars, but not a vehicle in sight. Also no animals, no children. But at least an acre of land—in the front, a multicolored splash of flowers, and in back, as I discovered later, a fertile, impeccably cultured fruit and vegetable farm. The place was so self-consciously well disposed, so flawlessly cultivated and maintained, that when I entered its gravitational pull, the glaring sunniness of its aura, I almost convulsed, broke into a fit of shakes and sprinted toward the gates in the direction of the churning, honks, slams, fog, and filthy crap of the city.

There was no corny, New Age name for this place, or the group of people residing here. No "Elysium" or "Valhalla." It was just some guy's house.

His name was Stephen Flanders. He was the first person, after Mary, that I met there, and everything about him starting with his name was uncomfortably charismatic. Stephen was about forty, a small man, maybe five foot six, but tanned like a lifeguard, cut like a featherweight boxer. His eyes appeared to be silver. It probably said "gray" on his driver's license. But gray didn't begin to do justice to their metallic sting. Two polished dimes dotted in the middle with a single drop of Indian Ink. Aluminum with tiny holes cut into the center. Little sterling planets. Mercury. Stephen's eyes were a bad poet's day out.

The other thing I immediately liked about Stephen was that he didn't have a beard. I seemed to have peculiar relations with bearded men.

I could imagine it would have been quite easy to fall in love with Stephen. I liked and trusted him from day one. But it didn't happen. As it turned out, Stephen was already in love with somebody else.

I met everybody in the house by way of a touchy-feely ritual that involved getting up hideously early in the morning, usually with the sun. I hadn't seen the sun heave itself up over the horizon since my speed-snorting days, and back then it was just an oversized yellow traffic light, illuminating my state of limbo. Not quite at rest, yet not ready to go. Sometimes, up here in the country, it glided slowly over the hills trailing gorgeous veils of deep red behind it, vast washes of orange, until the space above the mountains was filled with some kind of beautiful tropical juice spill in the sky.

There were seven people in the house at the time, and I met with one a day, so it took a neat and significant week.

Stephen talked to me first. We faced each other in the kitchen, palms pressed downward on the wood of the kitchen table. This was his big introduction. His welcome breakfast. The rest of the "group" had been sent outside or left upstairs to work on one of the three bathroom ceilings, whose quaint, pink paint was peeling like sunburnt skin and in need of a strip down and a new coat. There was all kinds of work, most of it self-perpetuating. The garden, the cooking, and the weekly trip to Ben Lomand to sell fruit and vegetables. They would take Stephen's truck, which he parked at the back of the house, perhaps so as not to ruin the self-sufficient, hippy facade for incoming guests.

"If you can pitch in, you are more than welcome to stay here for as long as you want," Stephen said. "Mary speaks very highly of you."

"Mary doesn't know me very well."

"I was raised on a commune," he went on, sipping creamy coffee from a thick, misshapen clay mug that look as though it had been handmade in kindergarten. "In Marin, just outside of Mill Valley, in the early seventies. I was home schooled between the ages of four and twelve, along with three other kids in the house. My sister, and our mom's friend's daughter, Margot. It would have continued through adolescence, but I don't think our parents could deal with all that pubescent energy around the house all day and all night, too. More than that, they couldn't remember chemistry, trigonometry, and calculus.

"So I was bussed off to Redwood High School, at which point I wished to God I'd been taught in a school along with regular kids in the first place. It wasn't that we were behind. If anything we were fields ahead. Spewing annoying pseudo-philosophical, half-baked intellectual adultspeak about Marx and Sartre and David Hockney while the rest of the kids discussed Blue Oyster Cult and the SATs.

"But socially we got our asses kicked. The girls hid my sister's clothes after PE and put them in the middle of the playing field so that she had to go out and get them after gym class, dripping wet with only a towel on at two in the afternoon. I wrote term papers for kids who promised to pay me, then they reneged on the deal and threatened to turn me in instead. My locker mate filled my backpack with itching powder. I broke out in flaming, puce lumps that itched, and wept so much I was taken to the emergency room on the day of my Algebra final, so that I missed the whole thing and had to make up the test on a hot Sunday morning.

"Living with others, sharing the burdens of sustaining each other, I still think it can work. But with limitations. You won't see any kids here. Kids, teenagers especially, rarely dig experimental, progressive parental values. Why should they? They're bullshit.

"I'm a Silicon Valley refugee. Former director of sales at Ascient.com. It was a stupid name. Nobody could pronounce it, fewer people could spell it to find their way to our site—and it had no meaning. If anything, it translates as 'Without knowledge,' which is quite fitting, now that I think about it. Along with the fact that it has 'ass' in the first syllable, when you say it out loud. Maybe it described us pretty well. But it didn't even describe what we were trying to do, which, in retrospect, was a thousand times more stupid than our name. Well, we did nothing. Nobody used us. We dug ourselves a twelve-million-dollar virtual grave and filed chapter eleven, and a couple of other chapters, too. I forget which ones. Six, four. Whatever they are.

"People still assume I'm a dot-com millionaire, just because I hung around in the 408 area code. It has a branding effect. People think I sold my stocks at their pinnacle, cashed out, bought this house, and turned overnight into a born-again hippy, ready to lay back, love, and live off the land.

"The fact is, my dad died and left me all his money. After the Marin commune broke apart under the strain of a couple of divorces in the eighties, he got into real estate. Buying and selling, buying and selling like an asshole. It's pretty lucrative. He had twelve and a half million dollars. My mom had long ago hightailed it off to Sweden with an industrial engineer, so he willed it all to me. This house is all I bought. Do you like it?"

On day two I met with Margot. She made me granola and a funny yogurt drink that tasted like something that might have dripped out from between my legs, only flavored with strawberries. Margot was a lean, elegant woman, with a tumbleweed of gray-black hair and bifocals. She walked with a cane and moved around with the hand and head tremors of someone much older.

"I suffer from multiple sclerosis, which is a disease of the brain and spinal cord." It was the first thing she said to me, as if that, alone, defined her.

Margot sucked in a mouthful of her homemade drink, leaving pale pink mucus on the patch of fine white hair above her lip.

"My nerves are scarred," she went on. "Well. Yes. Everybody here thinks their nerves are scarred. But mine really are. That's what MS is."

"What does it feel like?" I asked her, picking sunflower seeds from beneath my teeth.

"Nothing . . ." she said. "Numbness, weakness, dizziness, fatigue. You probably think you know what that's like, too. But you don't."

It did sound familiar. But I didn't argue with her.

"I'm in remission this month. Except for the shaking. It comes. It goes. It'll probably kill me in the end. I'll slip away one afternoon, in a garden chair in the orchard out back, a silly, quivering old jelly with a great head of hair, like Jackie du Pre, but without the talent. Well, I played the harp."

I wiped a drip of milky pink stuff from my chin.

"That's an unusual and romantic instrument," I said.

"An unwieldy and expensive instrument," said Margot. "We sold it to pay bills when I was a kid. Not 'we.' She. My mother. Right when I was sixteen, and I was just getting good. My dad ran off back to Sweden with another woman. We lived too close together. Something like that was bound to happen."

She was second-generation commune, too. Like Stephen.

"So you lost your harp, and got your ass kicked in high school," I said.

Margot tilted her head to the side, birdlike and curious, and for a moment she stopped shaking.

"I didn't get my ass kicked in high school!" she said. "I was enormously popular. Wherever did you get that idea?"

On Wednesday, I met with Ted. Suitably named Ted, whose plump, furry limbs and tummy made me think of a toy bear.

Ted told me he was a former gambling addict.

"You know what the difference between gambling addiction and drug dependency is?" he asked, in a quiet, paternal tone. "Nothing. You shake, you sweat, you lose weight, you lose friends, you lose money, you lose everything. You become violent. At my worst I flew to Reno using my boyfriend's credit card number, every other day. Sometimes winning, coming back for a day of twitching and hand-wringing at my teaching job, then flying out the next day, blowing my wad tenfold, and refusing to leave the Casino until I'd meted out my revenge against the monster. It was an animal, a giant, formidable silver and gold beast that lived and breathed and chinged and clattered in my head, rewarding, then robbing me, giving and taking, beating me, then showering me again with wealth and hope. When I got down to my last few bills, I'd have as many free drinks as possible, and just play slot machines until it was all gone. I used to have these terrible panic attacks when the change machine wasn't working. 'Empty when lit,' it said. Just like me.

"It took everything I had. My lover, my half of the house I shared with him, my job, my health, my mind. A good deal of my hair." He rubbed the few strands combed sideways across his crown.

"I won't stay here forever," he said, "It's a distraction, this mission. Is there waffle syrup dripping down my chin?"

Nicole was a nurse, like Mary. A slender blonde in her late twenties. A few months ago she had returned from post-Ceausescu Romania, where she'd worked in an orphanage, one of a number of underfunded bureaucratic organizations struggling to subsist after the breakup of the Soviet bloc, while the various other ill-fitting puzzle pieces of the Balkan regions gnawed violently at each others' edges.

"I wanted to bring a child back with me," she told me, looking into her poached eggs. "Did you know we farm them out the back?"

I looked out the kitchen window, expecting to spot a paddock filled with Eastern European toddlers rolling and playing in the grass.

"Not kids, of course," Nicole explained. "Sorry, I always do that. Listening to me is like tuning in a radio. I'm all over the dial. I meant eggs. We have chickens. Hens. Fresh eggs. You'll probably be on egg detail some morning soon if you stick around. But anyway, you have to have money. Not for the eggs. For the children. You can actually buy children from Eastern Europe. After Ceausescu, Americans were paying off Romanian families, offering bribes. Even when it's done legally, adoption is actually still a purchase. You can get them over the Internet now."

A drop of egg yolk slid down Nicole's elbow, and she dabbed at it with her cotton napkin.

"Disgusting," she said, though it wasn't quite clear whether she was referring to her table manners or the Romanian trade in orphaned children.

"You'd think it would be free, wouldn't you? I mean you're doing somebody else a favor and you pay *them*? I saw my fair share of crossed eyes, cleft palates, and club feet. Those kids come cheaper. Kids with dark hair come cheaper than blond ones. Siblings cheaper than single babies. Toddlers cheaper than newborns. And once a kid reached double digits . . ." She paused, and looked at her plate, pressing her fork into a pillow of mashed potato. "There was this one kid, a little boy . . . the parents came out from America expecting a healthy child. But he'd been born dead and resuscitated. He'd had in utero pneumonia, a brain hemorrhage, and was paralyzed below the waist. So, of course, they didn't want him. They sued for adoption fraud instead. I think they took home about

two hundred grand instead of the child. I just never under-
stood it."

She shrugged, sighed, and slumped down, shaking her head.

"I don't know," she said. "I think they would have been
better scrambled with some ham."

Cindy, who I met on Friday, would run every morning. I had
noticed her from the window of my pine loft bedroom,
where I rolled awake on my mattress and opened the shades
to see her jogging gracefully down the hill, in very short
shorts. Sometimes I'd watch her running home, often an
hour or an hour and a half later, still energized, still making
long, springy strides.

Cindy was twenty-two, with a philosophy degree from
Columbia in New York, or so she said. She was also a carbo-
hydrates fanatic, and ate mounds of oats for breakfast, with
water instead of milk, while I chewed on peanut butter toast
and licked at my hot chocolate.

"I wasn't always like this," she told me. Everybody seemed
to say that. "You should have known me in high school. I was,
like, totally unenlightened. I mean, I was like on fifteen kinds
of antidepressants, but didn't know what a head shop was."

"What changed you?"

"Um—" she looked away from me. "Um, getting away
from my parents, I guess. Um—living alone."

"I've seen you running in the morning. You keep quite a pace."

"I was on the track team in high school."

"Most people don't keep up with it."

"Well, it wasn't that long ago. Well, I mean, it was, but— you know . . ."

I didn't quite know, and she looked down into her bowl, exposing the dark roots of her short, dyed blond hair. Her hair looked a bit silly, so eggy and yellow, mismatched as it was with her cork-colored skin and black brows.

Cindy didn't seem to want to reveal much about herself. For all her talk of enlightenment, her eyes searched the room uneasily as though she were still a little lost.

On Saturday I hung out alone with Mary. It was the first moment by ourselves since I'd arrived at the house. The entire rest of the group had taken the truck to town to shop for the week, and we found ourselves drifting around the house alone like a couple of dust bunnies, before we sat and faced each other and made searing eye contact over hot drinks.

There was nothing to say. Mary simply walked around to my side of the table and hugged me hard. There was still little meat on me, and I felt as though I might bow and snap like a bare tree.

"Thanks for inviting me," I said. "I needed a break from all that shit I was doing."

"Me, too" she said.

"Your new friends are weirdos and fuckups," I said.

"Yeah," she said, "but you'll learn more."

She got all Mary the Mysterious on me at that point. I preferred the old Mary, but we ate better here.

And then there was John. I met him on a Sunday, and it might have been the closest thing I'd ever had to a religious experience outside of Christmas morning when my mother was still alive. John looked like a Sunday school depiction of Jesus Christ, with beautiful eyes and shoulder-length brown locks. He did not, however, have a beard, although it looked like one was coming in, which could only mean trouble.

"Volleyball?" he asked.

"Is there a net?"

"U. New Hampshire?" He was reading the emblems on my chest.

"Salvation Army special," I explained. Why was he looking *there*?

"I see you went to Princeton," I said, reading his.

"I didn't," he said, handing me a cup of coffee. "It's just part of my Universities I Didn't Go To sweatshirt collection. Along with Oxford, Harvard, Vassar . . . I thought it would attract women when I was out jogging. Until I realized jogging wasn't the best place to meet people. You know, you just sort of run past each other, everybody's trying to improve on their time and nobody wants to stop."

"Well, we're here now," I said.

"And what do you think?"

"I think I'll stay awhile," I said. "I needed a rest."

After all, I told myself, life was long. Or even if it wasn't it was a good enough excuse for not getting on with the things you were supposed to do.

"And how do you like the people you've met? Why do you think they are here?"

"Because they need freedom."

"Wrong. Because they need structure. Because human life is like paint splattered going all directions at once. Put a frame around it and you have the full picture. You can give it a name and people stop to admire and assess it."

Jesus, he's a bigger bullshitter than I am, I thought.

"Like a Jackson Pollock," I remarked, humoring him.

John laughed. I wanted him to say something in acknowledgment of Jackson. But he became quiet and leaned forward, gently but rather officially, like a doctor, or school principal. I leaned back.

"Mary told me you were a prostitute," he said.

"Mary said that? Mary called me that? I've never been called that in my life!"

"Were you?"

"I never worked the street," I said.

"It doesn't matter," he said flatly. He said everything flatly, like he was conducting a cross-examination or lie detector test, "You could have caught something nasty."

"I already had something nasty. Hepatitis B. I've had it since I was sixteen. You have it forever, I think."

"Oh, I know," he said. "As a matter of fact, I had it, too."

"Really!" I answered with perverse enthusiasm. "Good. Then we can't give it to each other."

He was silent again, and then he smiled. "Stephen doesn't encourage that kind of relationship between people in the group," he said. "Something in his childhood."

I don't know what it was in John's stiffness that appealed to me. I guess I just wanted to break him down—out of sheer mischief, like wanting to flash your tits from the audience at the actor performing Hamlet.

"What do people here think about me?" I asked.

"Don't know yet. I know what I think."

I'd meant him anyway.

"You strike me as a little bit narcissistic," he said.

"A little bit?" I snorted, "I totally am. But I love that about myself."

"You're a piece a work," he said dryly, and refilled my coffee cup without asking me first whether I wanted more.

I didn't like John at first. He had this awful military academy vibe and a chess champion coolness about him that I couldn't stand. His was the voice of reason that made everything out of my mouth so stupid and unreasonable. Well, it was. I should have thanked him for turning me on to that, I suppose. Yet, no matter what I said, he listened and nodded and tended, or at least pretended, to agree.

We started a tomato-growing project together in the back garden, every morning performing this ruse, this pastoral charade where we'd pretend that we knew what we were doing, watering the soil where someone else had planted the fruit, touching the leaves as if we really had any effect on their progress.

John stood in the sunshine, staring earnestly at the plants, while a spider carefully descended a thin shimmer of thread.

"It's strange to think," he said to me, watching the spider's progress, "the whole dot-com tech boom is clicking away just a few ugly freeways away in Silicon Valley while we stand around in the garden growing vegetables like a couple of peaceniks."

"What do you mean, *like* a couple of peaceniks?"

He laughed. He often laughed when I spoke, whether what I said was meant to be funny or not.

"Look," I added, softly gesturing toward the perfect geometry of the cobweb stretched between leaf and stalk. *"That's* a web. Not some crap on a computer."

John rolled his eyes at my uninspired corniness.

"Don't worry about it ," he said, squeezing the fruit. "It's a fad. It'll soon be over. I've always thought the Internet was the CB radio of the nineties."

"Except CB radio users weren't such assholes."

"Stupid names though. Big Ben to Snow Cat, or whatever."

"But they weren't all young and arrogant," I said. "Fucking nineteen-year-old internet CEOs. Never trust anyone under thirty! That's what I say."

"I'm under thirty," John said.

"So am I. Obviously." I pulled an overripe tomato from the vine, and a squirt of juice and seeds exploded from a fissure in the wrinkly skin, sliding down my forearm.

"Steady," John said, and he stepped in, and wiped my wrist with the sleeve of his sweatshirt.

I looked toward my dusty sneakers.

"My dad had a CB Radio," I said.

The annoying thing about John—one of the annoying things, aside from the fact that he was so good looking—was that he questioned me incessantly about my own life, revealing little of his own. Maybe it was because whatever he started to talk about, I couldn't wait for him to finish a sentence before I would start to talk about myself and wouldn't shut up. He didn't seem to mind, but he should have. He should have told me to shut up and listen. Somebody should have said that to me a long time ago.

We lay on our backs on the grass one afternoon, exhausted after washing the household bedsheets by hand in the back garden hot tub, manually wringing them and hanging them out to dry on an old-fashioned washing line strung up between two trees.

Out of nowhere, staring at the sky, he said, "I have a graduate degree in mathematics from the University of Massachusetts."

"Tom's a mathematician," I said.

"Who's Tom again?" he asked.

"My dad!"

"Tom? Why don't you just call him 'Dad'? That's so phoney."

"I didn't inherit those skills at all," I said. "I detested it when he brought home pages of numbers. I hate numbers."

"*Hate* numbers?" he said, rolling over onto his stomach to laugh at me.

"Yes," I continued, not sharing the joke, "because when most people look at pages of numbers, they represent money. To me, they represent nothing."

"Only if you multiply everything by zero."

"Oh shut up," I said. "I fucking hate them. If I had to choose between numbers and prison, I'd choose prison. If I had to choose between math and death, I'd choose death."

He rolled onto his back and started cracking up again, his concave lower torso shuddering up and down, his T-shirt sliding up a little to reveal the ribbon of dark hair reaching downward from his navel.

"That's bold," he said.

"Not really," I answered. "I believe in reincarnation."

I wasn't sure if I did believe in reincarnation. I'd never really thought about it before. But it was as though I'd never had a proper talk with anyone in my entire adult life, and all my half-baked, idealistic bullshit spilled out on top of John. Because I thought I didn't like him much, it didn't matter what he thought.

"What do you want to come back as?" John asked.

"Oh, a gay guy for sure. Look for me in the year 3002. I'm in leather."

"A gay man?"

"Sure. That way I get to have men and be one."

"And what do you want to be in this life?"

"Oh God." I rolled my eyes, "If I knew that, I wouldn't be here."

"Not a hooker."

"Why do you keep calling me that?"

He took hold of my shoulders, looked me in the eyes, raised his eyebrows, then let go and gazed back up at the clouds.

I blew out a breath of air and laced my hands over my hips.

"I was in it for the money," I said.

"You're better than that."

"Obviously not."

"You know what you are? You're a social climber, climbing in the wrong direction."

"Maybe I'd like to be a writer," I suggested.

I didn't know if I really wanted to be a writer, either. But it was something to tell him. I felt a little embarrassed. It sounded funny and pretentious, like calling your own dad by his first name.

But John didn't laugh at that at all. "You'd be good at that," he said.

"Oh, no," I said, as though he'd just sentenced me. "That's a terrible thing to say. People view writing as some sort of search for spiritual truth. I'm inclined to think it's more about taking the truth, taking human nature and dressing it up and putting a spin on it. I think it's really more about being a good liar."

"In that case, maybe I should try it myself."

"What do you mean by that?" I asked.

He paused, waiting for my question to float off, then went on. "I think you'd be better than most people."

"Why? Because I'd make a better liar than most people?"

"No. Because you suffer from human nature more than most people."

I turned to look at him to see if he was serious or shitting me, and saw that his eyes were closed now, his arms stretched out over his head. There was an inch gap between his abdomen and the waist of his jeans. I rolled onto my front next to him, and slipped my palm down into the space. John didn't move. He just lay there as though in a pleasant sleep. I slid my hand out again, rolled over onto my back, and closed my eyes, too.

The sheets on the washing line flapped over our heads, sprinkling us with cold, soap-scented water.

"When I close my eyes," I said, "I don't see black anymore. I see space."

He started laughing again.

"Prick," I muttered.

"What did you say?"

"I said you're a prick."

The other annoying thing about John was how much I really liked him.

For a while, we dodged and danced around each other. We were never a team of three men and a gang of four women. Not six couples with one leader. We were a group of seven individuals who didn't ask too many direct questions and never gave straight answers.

It worked well, and we really did share the burdens of self sufficiency with restraint and discipline. Stephen would drive off to nearby Felton for normal products: Detergent, Band-Aids, shampoo, chocolate.

We were each assigned to cook for the others on a given night of the week. Margot excelled at homemade pasta and lemon soufflé. Cindy was dreadful at everything, cheating with canned chili and mammoth quantities of mashed potatoes. She could never gauge how many potatoes it took to feed seven, always cooking too few, then adding mayonnaise to the starchy, lumpy mess in order to stretch it a little further.

Stephen supposedly made beer in the basement, although I never saw anyone drinking it. Mary nursed us through the occasional stomachache or flu bout. Ted pruned trees, weeded, and organized late-night poker games played for sugar-free chocolate-covered raisins. John mended the truck with a little help from the manual, and the rest of the time he generally tormented me with aloof flirtations.

It was perfect, for a while. But I eventually learned that, like a nice piece of fruit, it would only be sweet and appealing for a limited time.

The starter eventually fell ill on Stephen's Toyota. John, having become the designated mechanic, coasted off down the hill into town one morning to get it fixed. I was left to tackle our shared chore of laundry alone that day. With all his surplus cash, I didn't see why Stephen couldn't have sprung for a washer and dryer inside the house, and then we could have used the hot tub for relaxation and parties, like normal people.

Instead, it was our clothes and linen, not our bodies, that were treated to a 220-gallon wood-finished spa, with nineteen hydrojets, a slipsteam weir filter, automatic brominator, and ten air injector jets with aromatherapy delivery.

That day we were out of laundry detergent, and I threw in three bars of cheap hand soap from the kitchen. When they floated to the top, not melting, I returned with a fourth, which I grated into the water with a cheese grater until rewarded with a satisfactory lather.

I left the laundry in the suds with the jets on for about ten minutes, then drained the tub, filled it again with cold, drained it again, and finally stomped on the sodden mass in my bare feet for about another quarter hour, to try to get the excess water out. After that, I heaved the clammy, heavy mounds of fabric into a series of plastic baskets, dragged them over to the washing line and hung them up in the fresh air. And for all the hard work, there still something quite wholesome about being slapped in the face for your efforts by the lavendar scented, wet cotton blowing in the wind.

I slung the sheets and towels over the line, fastening the corners with old-fashioned wood and wire clothespins. Clipping the last edge of a towel onto the line, I somehow closed the peg onto my index finger, pinching the skin between the wood and the metal spring, drawing blood. I twisted my hand into the hem of my T-shirt and headed back inside.

The wood floors and carpeted stairs were baked in that heavy warmth and stillness that fills a place after the sun has poured in for a few hours, and nobody is around to stir up the air. I reached the top of the stairs and turned right into the bathroom. Washing away the blood, I doused my cut in some tea tree oil and covered the cut with a bandage.

I looked in the mirror of the bathroom cabinet. I'd been at Empire Grade a month, and the yellow pall had gone from my skin. My teeth and the whites of my eyes appeared magazine bright now, against my newly acquired tan.

As I turned away to go back outside and fetch the baskets, I heard a noise from the back of the house. At first it sounded like mewing, like a kitten trapped somewhere, trying to paw its way from under a blanket. But as it grew louder, it seemed to be the voice of a girl crying. I left the bathroom and, moving towards these muted weeping noises, I realized it was coming from the rear bedroom. Stephen's room.

His door was ajar. And I stood dumbly in the quiet of the hall as he tumbled about on his bare mattress, smelling her hair, stroking the smooth, shiny surface of her shin bone. He rolled aside for a moment, onto his back. She lifted a leg over his torso, smiling, pulling her hair away from her face, then leaning in to put her tongue in his mouth. It was Stephen and Cindy.

I watched stupidly for a very short time, then walked away, wondering why I should feel such disappointment and sadness at somebody else's pleasure.

Nicole had made some kind of leek frittata and raspberry bread pudding for dinner. They opened a bottle of Merlot and toasted to Ted, who had just announced that he was one year free of his gambling habit. Margot extolled the virtues of yoga, which she had begun to practice each morning, and had noticed a marked improvement in the physical symptoms of her MS. I stared through the dining room door, and noticed the fridge, singing away in the dark kitchen. I tried to imagine the reaction of the group were they suddenly to find it filled with Kentucky Fried Chicken and cheap American beer. I looked at the "Horse Country" calendar, half mistaking the "1997" heading for "1970."

And then I glanced over at John, and noticed he was looking at me. But John looked at everyone. He sat quietly at mealtimes, watching one face at a time, as though auditioning us for play he would later direct, or monitoring a focus group from behind a one-way glass screen.

My bedsheets were crisp, rigidly clean, and slightly scaly. Flakes of grated soap had fused to them as they'd dried. Lying in the dark, I scratched scented white stuff from the folds of the bed with the edge of my toenails. My eyes fell closed and I saw suds and trees, blood and bread, sugar and milk, wine and slot machines, and finally I saw nothing.

"Shh," I heard myself say, minutes or hours later. "Shh," I said in my sleep.

My door had creaked open, bringing with it a warm blade of light from the hall, and John, dressed in sweatpants, socks, and no shirt. He tiptoed in.

"What did you do to the bed linen?" he demanded in frantic whisper. "It feels like there's poison oak in the bed."

"Do your own fucking laundry, then," I mumbled into my pillow. "I'm not your fucking wife."

John said nothing, but he didn't move. So I just lay there, pretending to be asleep, waiting for him to go away.

"You've got your clothes on," he said.

I'd been so tired after dragging the laundry around, and four cups of chamomile tea, I'd fallen onto my mattress fully dressed.

"Oh. Thanks," I said.

"Ah. So, you're not asleep."

"What do you want?"

And he sat down on the edge of my mattress, placed his hand gently behind my head, and kissed me. I reach up and pulled him down. He smelled of wine and girly lavender from the soap I'd used for the wash.

I wriggled out from beneath the sheets and slowly I peeled off my shirt and pulled off my jeans.

"Oh God. Sorry," I said. "Look at that."

"What?"

"My underwear and bra. Black cotton bottoms, lacy white top. They don't match at all."

"I hope you're kidding," he said.

"No, really, they don't."

We had sex carefully and quietly. I was finally able to put aside my screaming pornographic histrionics, my elaborate showmanship, my panting, breathing, overdramatized vocalization of fake gratification. That night I was finally able to stop "doing it." It was as though all the pleasure I was hoping for in life was coming to me all at once on that one night. But I guess it was just the one time. It never happened like that again.

We slept together until morning, and awoke tangled up in limbs and hair.

During the night, I had turned away from John, and I woke up with my back toward him. But he had wrapped his arms around my waist, rested his head on my back and shoulders. It felt so unfamiliar, so close that one of us should have stopped breathing, and the other breathed for both of us. I didn't feel like I could inhale or exhale at all without causing a huge disturbance or stealing oxygen away from him.

In the quiet hours of daybreak, I suddenly recalled being told, as a child, never to climb into a refrigerator, because you couldn't get out. At the time, I had wondered why you couldn't just push the door open again from the inside. I had wondered why you'd want to climb into a fridge in the first place. The wisdom behind this, I now realized, was that you would want to pretend the fridge was something else. A vessel to take you away, or a home where you lived. And then it would fall over, door to floor, when no one was watching, and you'd suffocate.

John's rib cage pushed into me and pulled away as he breathed in and out. My instinct was to slide away, wash myself in cold water, and leave him sleeping alone. You can't live that close all day long, all year round. Facedown on top of each other, with your feet in the vegetable drawer and your head up by the icebox.

Before I could move, he began to speak.

"Who's Abigail?" he asked, before he even knew whether I was awake.

"Abigail?"

"You were calling out to her in your sleep last night. Do you always talk in your sleep?"

"I don't know," I said. "Nobody's ever spent the whole night with me before."

Typically, just as everything was beginning to fall so beautifully together, something would fall away. I might as well have been living in a sand castle. A violent wave would always sweep in, then recede, and a chunk of silver and gold sand would crack and drop off, ruining everything.

Nobody else had woken up. It all happened in that nebulous time zone between night and morning, dark and light, when the spirit of just about everything seems half dead, like a drowning victim before the mouth-to-mouth, before coughing and jerking reluctantly to life for another twenty hours of existence. The pulse of the day would usually start with the birds, one chirping stubbornly after another to coax the world into its inevitable rhythm.

But that morning there was no birdsong, no gentle kiss of life. We were slapped awake, quite viciously. John and I were the only ones who heard and saw it. The scraping of car tires on the gravel in front of the house. The chaos of footsteps on the stairs, the cries, the clamor of limbs and the struggle in the doorway.

We rushed towards Mary's room in the front of the house, looking onto the drive below.

Mary wasn't in her room. Her bedclothes were spilling from the mattress to the floor. A tipped-over juice glass rolled toward us on the hard wood floor, spreading in its wake a pool of violent orange. John and I looked from her window to see a childlike figure in pajamas and a gray haired man with a cigarette in his mouth holding the top of her tiny, white arm. Next to him stood a fierce, redheaded woman. At first glance I thought it was Mary. She had the same pale, crepe paper skin and fruity green eyes. But this woman was much older, her voice much harsher and deeper as she shouted and pleaded with the girl in pajamas. We saw it through glass, heard it all played out in muted tones, like watching the entire scene at the drive-in with the speaker blown out. Eventually, the figure in pajamas turned her head. Her mouth opened but nothing came out. Her eyes blinked strangely, repeatedly, but she appeared so disabled by shock that there were no tears. I sprang back from the window, ready to fly downstairs, to kick and fight and intervene. But John grasped my hand and pulled me back.

"No, Juliet," he said. "Let them go."

And we stood by, upstairs, in her bedroom, and watched as Mary's mother and father pushed her stunned body into the backseat of their Volvo and took her home.

S p o i l e d

I was no longer Mary's friend. That is, with Mary gone, I was no longer "Mary's friend." I asked myself almost every day what we all were doing there. The mistake I made was that I didn't ask anyone else. And at this stage, it didn't matter. Nothing mattered, actually, because I was In Love. Love, as they say, is blind, so you go stumbling about knocking things over, hurting yourself and having any number of messy spills. As if I didn't have enough of those with 20/20 vision.

Despite our isolation from the outside world, everybody at Empire Grade took a healthy interest in current affairs, and whoever was sent into town was mandated to return with a handful of the day's newspapers. Not just the local paper, but preferably the *New York* or *Los Angeles Times,* at least, and often *The Economist, Harper's,* and *The Nation* as well.

It was late afternoon, and John swung above me in the backyard hammock as I lay under it, my hands reaching up to the heavy curve of canvas, pushing him back and forth as he read the Sunday *Chronicle.*

"You've got to love this, Juliet," he said to the sky. "Ten milk jugs full of gasoline were found on the roof of a Nike shop in a mall in Minnesota. Apparently snow dampened all the fuses, so it didn't go off."

"And am I supposed to love the milk jugs or the snow?" I wondered aloud.

He didn't answer.

I scooted out from beneath the swaying hammock and lay on the grass beside him, lacing my hands in front of my eyes, allowing a slim shaft of sun through my fingers.

"Did you know the first word I ever learned to say was 'light'?"

"How awesome. That has almost a holy quality to it," John said.

"Actually, I had a cigarette in my mouth," I said.

He rolled out of the hammock and lay beside me on the grass. We were always lying next to each other now, John and I. We seemed to speak more honestly when looking straight up instead of at each other. I was never fully sold on that whole direct-gaze thing. Eye contact was for people *not* being straight— motivational speakers and stereo salesmen. Live nude girls.

"I don't know anything about your childhood," he said.

"I was the same as I am now, only smaller."

"I find the older I get, the more I think about the past.

Sometimes I'm completely overwhelmed with sadness and longing. I just can't stop it."

"Me, too," I agreed. "I'm way more nostalgic than I used to be."

Love may be blind, but it is a temporary condition. And soon enough the blindfold began to slip. I started to observe things, and I began to sense that some of the household members were talking in my absence. Stephen, Ted, and Nicole were particularly guilty. They'd fall silent sometimes when I'd enter a room. Even John was doing it.

One evening, as I was helping Cindy prepare for dinner, I agreed to tidy the dining room and put out the place settings. As usual, the table was covered with a number of papers, envelopes, and various flyers. Stephen collected the mail from a post office box in Ben Lomand about once a week. It was always bills and junk mail, which he'd toss onto the dining room table until somebody moved it aside, sorted through, and threw the unsolicited garbage into the recycling.

I scraped the entire stack into the crook of my forearm and went to put them into the cardboard box beside the trash can, next to the kitchen sink. As I dropped them in, one of the magazines slid from my arm onto to the floor. I reached down to retrieve it and placed it in the box. And as I stuck it on the top of the pile, I noticed, partially covered in the mound of papers, an unopened envelope. It was on green stationery and handwritten, addressed to me.

Cindy cursed to herself at the stove, spilling dry pasta shells into the gas flame, her back to me as I pulled out the envelope, slid it down the front of my jeans, and headed for the stairs.

The postmark was June 15, two weeks ago. I lay on my bed and put the pretty, emerald paper flat on my pillow.

> *Dear Juliet,*
>
> *First, please pack up the rest of my belongings and mail them to me at the return address in San Francisco.*
>
> *Second, I think you should leave Empire Grade soon. I have to be careful what I write because I'm afraid Stephen will open this. I understand his values, but he is a little paranoid. You'll find out.*
>
> *Mary*

Cindy had made a cement-like potato and pasta dinner and a flaccid blackberry bread pudding for dessert. She was always "carbo loading" us, like we were at a triathlon training camp.

"I *starve* if I don't have them," she said once. "It's the running."

Cindy was skinnier than I was, so either it was that, or she was still growing.

About halfway through dinner they ran out of wine.

"No problem," Nicole announced, scraping back her chair. "I think there's another bottle in the basement."

"I'll get it," I offered.

They all looked at their plates. There followed a chilly silence, the whole scene like some gothic freeze-frame from a Hammer Horror movie.

"You don't know where the basement is," Stephen said.

"I didn't know there *was* a basement."

"I'll go," said Ted. "It's horribly dark and dangerous down there."

That night I lay in bed and entertained morbid fantasies about mounds of heroin, suitcases of laundered money, rotting corpses piling up, rancid beneath the house. And then John came in and kissed my lids.

John heated up in the dark. He was warmer at night, kinder in bed, once he was naked. His intellect and asshole-ish sarcasm came off with his clothes. I never called out or squeaked or panted anymore. Afraid to make noise we just breathed and sighed as though we'd gingerly stepped together into a nice hot bath.

He'd lie with me for about an hour, sometimes slipping into sleep, the rise and fall of his chest below the covers slowing and deepening as he drifted off. But he'd always wake up, kiss my head like a parent, and go back to his room. That night, though, I grasped his wrist as he sat up and pulled away from me.

"Why can't you ever stay?"

"I can't sleep in here."

"You were asleep. Wake up with me."

"I just did."

"Tomorrow."

"I don't want the others to know. It would be hypocritical."

He had put his T-shirt back on and had returned to his cautious, clinical self.

"Is that you talking, or is that Stephen?"

"It's Stephen talking, and me nodding in agreement."

He stood up and walked toward the door.

"Stephen and Cindy are going at it, you know?" I said, "I caught them one afternoon. He did her in the ass, too."

He stopped in his tracks, rolled his eyes, ran his hands through his hair, and looked up toward the top of the door frame.

"Why didn't you tell me?"

"I thought it would be hypocritical," I said.

"That dirty bastard."

John took his shirt off again, climbed into bed, and rolled over, facing away from me.

"I thought this was a retreat, not a fucking monastery," I said.

"You thought this was a *retreat*? Do you think they advertise this in the back of yoga magazines? Christ, Juliet."

"What is it, then?"

"Well, it's not a retreat."

I rolled over aggressively, tearing the covers away from him selfishly. He yanked them back, and I pretended to have fallen asleep in less than thirty seconds just to avoid further argument.

Deeper into the night, I woke up, still unused to the extra body in my bed, scared of thrashing around, talking in my sleep again, snoring or kicking. I turned over. John was awake, staring at the thread of light between the door and the floor. He looked much older in the shadows, in the middle of the night, the darkness deepening the circles beneath his eyes, accentuating the creases in his brow. He looked angry and worried and tired. I should have just let him go back to his own room.

From the possessions left behind in her room, I came to know Mary better than I ever had by being around her.

I packed up her things with a melancholy nostalgia as though she were dead. With every object, every book, every odd sock, every sample sachet of cheap shampoo, I was left with a collage so broken up and abstract that it bore no relation to the Mary I thought I had known. The bits and pieces might as well have been the contents of the lost luggage of a total stranger, whose suitcase had been switched with mine on the baggage carousel.

Mary was a size two. She wore thong underwear, some of which had the label cut out of it, either because it had been purchased at a discount outlet, or because it itched, or because she wore it on porno shoots. She used sesame oil somewhere on her face or body, she took a nonprescription anti-inflammatory designed for back pain, and she suffered from athlete's foot. I wondered if she'd caught that from me.

She painted her nails with clear polish, used cheap hand lotion and organic tea tree oil mouthwash. She wore contact lenses, which I'd never noticed. She read *Gray's Anatomy,* apparently for pleasure. It was beside her bed, bookmarked with an unaddressed postcard to and from nobody, of Mount Fuji in Japan. She had read, or was going to read *Brave New World, The Day of the Triffids, A Tale of Two Cities, Rebecca, Don't Stop the Carnival, The Joy of Cooking, The Joy of Sex,* and *Slaughterhouse Five.*

Mary kept a personal journal, in which she'd written every day since October 1996. Shamefully, I leafed through, gleaning only brief headlines of each month's events, flipping through the pages as quickly as possible so that it would soon be over.

"Cleaner than a surgeon's thumbnail" . . . "Best job I ever had" . . . "I wouldn't be surprised if he's gay" . . . "Juliet is an introverted snob" . . . "And I could be risking my life or jail" . . . "Why can't we be more like Canada?" . . . "So little wisdom, so much pain."

Mary had an autographed black-and-white photograph of the original Catwoman in her cat suit, signed in a black marker, "To Marie—Purrfect—Julie Newmar," and another of the eighties movie actor Corey Haim. She had a small collection of snapshots. There was a good one of her as a young child of about eight, dressed in a nurse's outfit, too big, so that it slipped off her shoulder. She was holding hands with a little boy dressed as Sherlock Holmes, his oversized hat all the way down to his

upper lip, and various women looking much like Karen Car-
penter and Rhoda, in bell bottoms, pendants, and head scarves,
frozen, candid, smoking or gesticulating in suspended anima-
tion in the background. There was her graduation photo from
nursing college. She looked heavier, softer in the cheeks, freckly
skin a fresh print, not yet faded by the agitating cycles of adult
life. There was a Polaroid of the Cherry Tree girls. Jasmine,
Sima, Mary, and me—Jasmine and Sima perfect and decorative
like they'd stepped, hand in hand, off the top of a cake; Mary
and I looking like a couple of tired old drag queens.

"So little wisdom, so much pain." After I closed the suitcase
and placed it in the middle of the rug, those words lingered in
the room as if they'd floated off and dripped themselves onto
the walls. I opened the case, retrieved the diary, and looked
for that phrase again. January 17th. Two A.M. It was a reference to a dental problem, her wisdom teeth, which had been
flaring up and causing discomfort to her gums at night.

John went back to sleeping in his own room. I'd finally gotten
used to the heat of his body in the bed, and now I missed it.

One night, I decided to try to sneak in with him. I crept
softly into the bathroom, dabbed a little water on my hair, some
lotion on my face, washed my feet, then walked down the hall
and gently pushed against his bedroom door. I planned to stand
disheveled and seductive in the doorway as he had done for me,

hoping he'd roll over, turn back his top sheet, and pat the mattress next to his hip. But, squinting into the deep gray of the room, I found that it was empty, the bed still neatly made.

I turned away and shuffled directly down the hall to the tiny corner room in the front of the house. There I heard deep, hushed sighs and shuffling of cotton and blankets, a low groan, a flicker of movement through the crack beneath the door. I knocked twice, briskly. Without waiting for an answer, I pushed the door inward, to the sound of a sharp squawk. Not the occupant, but the door creaking horribly on its hinges. There on the thin mattress against the far wall, I found Cindy, upsidedown, her legs over her head, head between elbows, feet kicked up against the wall in a rather impressive yoga pose. Her blond hair had flopped downward onto the floor, exposing the undergrowth of dark roots. On her back and shoulders, I notice a spray of tiny red, round dots, like a rash that had never quite healed.

She pushed her feet into the wall, kicking her legs down, and sat cross-legged on the sheets, cheerful and pink in the face.

"Juliet! Hi!"

"Sorry," I said. "I thought I heard a squawk. Like a bird."

"That was you opening the door."

"Well, never mind."

"No problem. I had my clothes on."

She looked terribly young, sitting there with her legs

crossed in her yellow flannel pajamas, flush and healthy. Quite a natural beauty, apart from the hair.

"I can't sleep on these sheets," she said. "They wash them in hippy soap, and they're brittle like paper."

"Is that what's wrong with your back? You look like you have a rash."

"It's not a rash," she said. "I've had that for a while."

"Is it a birthmark?"

"Scars."

"It looks like somebody flicked hot ash on you."

"My mom did it," she said.

I was about to launch into a lengthy interrogation, but she said, "It's over now. She was drunk. Forget it. Just get some decent laundry soap. And get us some soft toilet paper while you're there. That recycled stuff is like newspaper."

"You're telling me?" I moaned, "I'm clipping coupons and going to Save Rite."

"Great," whispered Cindy. "Don't tell Stephen, though. He wants to blow that place up."

I had been trotting down the hill for about twenty minutes before a car came along, a blue SUV driven by a woman. She came along the road behind me, honked, then pulled over and rolled down the window.

"Be careful on these curves, you'll get run over," she said. "Need a lift?"

"Thanks." I dragged myself into the passenger seat, which was so ridiculously elevated it was like climbing into a tractor.

"Whosat?" came a voice from behind us. I turned to see a toddler strapped into a child seat in the rear. She was blond like her mother, and she sucked on the spout of a plastic juice cup decorated with cartoon fruits with smiling faces.

"I'm Juliet," I said, making a tentative finger wave toward the child.

The woman put the car into gear and turned toward me, flipping her ponytail into her face.

"No kidding?" she said, pulling strands of hair from her mouth with a neatly manicured hand, "That's my name, too."

"No way! I never meet other Juliets."

"It's not a very common name in this country. More popular in England, I think. The whole Shakespearean thing."

"My mother was English."

"My dad was."

The girl in the back began tapping her cup against the window in time to the boy band R&B ballad oozing from the car radio.

"And this is Christina."

"How are you, Christina?" I asked into the rearview mirror.

"Free."

"Free?"

The other Juliet laughed, pulling her sunglasses from the top of her head as we rounded a corner into a blinding sheet of midafternoon sunshine.

"She thinks you said 'How old are you?'"

"Free and I laugh," said Christina, jerking her legs up and down against the upholstery.

"That's right," said her mother. "Three and a half."

Christina then let out a fearful squeal and began to cry and scream with such terror I thought for a second that some huge wild dog had leapt into the car and buried its teeth into her throat. But she had only dropped her cup onto the floor.

"I'm going all the way into Santa Cruz," said Juliet.

"That's perfect. I wanted to go into town," I said.

"You're lucky I stopped instead of some freak. Who knows what evil lurks in the Santa Cruz Mountains?"

In fact, I was starting to get some idea, which was why I'd elected to take a solo excursion that day, into town, to be among shoppers and students, smokers and sports fans. Also, to buy laundry detergent, and synthetic, chemical-based sunscreen, instead of health crap that didn't smell nice and didn't really work.

"What do you do?" she asked me, perhaps pegging me for a freak myself.

"I'm helping some friends renovate a house up here," I said,

suddenly wishing it were true, and wondering if even the
"friends" part had any veracity to it. "And you?"

"Teach fourth grade. Not much of a living. My husband's a
police officer."

"A *police*man? Wow."

"It's OK," she said, "It's not a disease."

Christina stopped crying and burst into an unseasonal round
of "Frosty the Snowman." We Juliets were quiet for a few minutes, but after a while I noticed, in my peripheral vision, that the
other Juliet was intermittently looking at me. Her eyes flickered
back and forth from the road to my face, constantly watchful, as
parents are, apparently waiting for me, too, to spill something,
or get my hand trapped in the car window and start bawling.

Eventually, I turned toward her and made eye contact as
she snuck another peek in my direction. She turned her eyes
back to the road, then to the rearview mirror.

"Sorry," she laughed, "You look familiar."

It didn't particularly surprise me. We probably went to
high school together. She was probably that volleyball player
with the tan.

"Are you an actress?" she asked.

"Oh no!" I laughed. "Well . . . who knows? Maybe."

"I'm sure I've seen your picture somewhere."

"Oh dear. Was I clothed?"

"I don't know," she continued. "Maybe you just look like
someone."

She dropped me off on Soquel Avenue. I stood on the sidewalk, waving at my own reflection in her sunglasses in the wing mirror. The other Juliet stuck her brown arm out and opened and shut her palm in a backwards wave. I half hoped Christina would turn around and gesture enthusiastically from the back window, but I realized she was strapped firmly in, facing front as they drove safely away.

I hadn't been to Santa Cruz since leaving town after college in early '95. Being home made me think of my parents. Not just my father, but my mother as well. It was a ridiculous, sentimental overreaction after only two years, but it did happen. The cheery, generic names on the street signs: Pennsylvania Avenue, Pine Street, peppered here and there with the Spanish ones—Cayuga, Benito. The smell of the air, the position of certain buildings and trees. I realized right then how much I really missed it. Not the town, but the *time*. Somehow, it was all so recent.

Save Rite was having their grand opening. They were giving away free scoops of ice cream and I ordered coconut cream sorbet and headed toward the laundry soap. At first I reached for the biodegradable, perfumeless goop in a plain white jug. But suddenly the neighboring brand called out to me seductively in screaming orange and flourescent blue. Like a chronic dieter succumbing to a junk food craving, I scooped it up and marched off to the sunscreen section, where I bought an expensive tube of something French and heavily perfumed in the same flavor as my melting sorbet.

Wandering past the cheap shoe section, I thought about getting some flip-flops, but they no longer carried the rubber, plain-colored variety. Instead they all seemed to have concrete soles covered in fake velvet, and straps made of neon plastic beads. I perused the nail polish for a moment, and thought about doing a toxic wall mural on the side of Stephen's house in their floridly named, crayon box colors.

A voice crackled over the intercom as I drifted off into chain store hypnosis.

"Manager to the monitor room," it called, crisply inter-rupting a muzak version of "Back in the USSR."

I thought about Sima for a moment, stealing that umbrella and crying in the backseat of her parents' car. And I thought of Mary, packed into the backseat in her pajamas. I thought of Christina sobbing in her car seat over her cup. And I thought of me, on the back of my dad's motorcycle, riding around the Santa Cruz Mountains on a Sunday afternoon, crying only from the cold wind blowing in my face.

God, I was spoiled.

I glanced over at an elderly man buying a Whitman's chocolate sampler and a packet of razors.

And that was all I did. I had another scoop of free ice cream—vanilla this time, and then I hitched a ride back with a quiet, older woman, a restaurant owner from Felton, my safe arrival somehow implicit in her gender and her colorless hair.

• • •

As I lay in bed, I wondered not whether John would come and have sex with me, but, like some fifties-era housewife, whether he would notice the pleasant, new Spring Fresh fragrance of the bedsheets. I rolled over to check my watch, which I usually kept inside my sandals on the floor beside me. Reaching down in the dark, I realized I'd left it down by the hot tub, where I'd taken it off to wash the sheets. I could have waited until morning, of course, but it was my mother's old watch and we were expecting rain.

The first drops of rain began to fall just as I turned back toward the house, my wristwatch tucked beneath my T-shirt. Looking up toward the house, about a hundred feet away, I noticed a soft rectangle of light coming from a window, low down at ground level. I was about to walk up to peer in and discover whether or not there was actually a gym, a card club, or a pool hall in the basement that nobody had told me about. But just as I started to walk up the wet grass, I heard a voice coming from behind me.

"Oh crap. It's raining. I've got to go."

Slowly turning around and searching the damp, gray air, I spotted John, leaning against the trunk of a tree, his right arm raised, hand by his ear. There he was, buried in darkness at the bottom of the garden, talking on a cell phone.

I felt an odd sense of embarrassment. It could not have been more dizzying had I discovered him masturbating, defecating, or having sex with a dog. Instead of confronting him, I ran away, as quietly as I could, back up towards the house.

Once inside, as I turned to the stairs, I could see that same yellow-white shade of light, this time coming from beneath the door in the hall, just before the kitchen—the door I'd originally assumed led to a closet. My watch, still ticking, said one-thirty-five. I walked over and grasped the handle. And just as I did so, there was a sharp, aggressive knock on the door. Not, I realized, the door I was facing, but the door behind me. The front door of the house. My hand sprung involuntarily, my body shivering like a wet dog. I stood still. The knock came again. Five echoey, uppercase knuckle wraps.

So I opened it. And there, standing in the dark, disheveled and quaking himself, was Dan McKenna.

"Thank God," he sobbed. "You *are* here! Where have you been?"

"Where have I been? Here. I'm here."

"I know that," he stumbled. "How do you think I found you?"

"I don't know. What's the matter? I'm here."

"Here? What's here?"

I realized, not for the first time, that I didn't know the answer to that question. And Dan wasn't waiting for a reply.

"Pack your bags," he barked. "Your father's been in an accident."

"I though he was in Pakistan."

"He's been back for three months. Everybody's been worried to death about you. We've filed a missing persons report . . . fliers on lamposts . . ."

His voice fell apart, his big speech collapsing into shards of breath and coughing. I just nodded, ran upstairs, and bulldozed my belongings—clothes, shoes, hairbrush, books, wallet, watch—into two large pillowcases. Not since the earthquake had I felt so much as though the whole house was crumbling and falling away around me as I stood helpless in the middle.

That is, more or less, what had happened.

Dan waited at the door, but as soon as he saw my over-stuffed bags he shook is head and waved his hands about in distraught semaphore.

"No no no no no! Less stuff. A small bag. I'm on the bike."

I ran back up to my room, dumped the pillowcases on the bed, and plunged my arm into them to retrieve my money and ID, a few clothes and underwear. I shoved them into my leather purse and stuffed it under my jacket.

Dan handed me a helmet, took my hand, and dragged me from the house. Lumpy and awkward, I sat like a sack of potatoes on the back of the bike as it growled ferociously and pounced off into the night. All the way down the twists of hill I wanted to talk. What? When? How bad is it? An entire soap opera of interrogatives played itself over and over in my head as he drove the bike down the hill, too fast for the rain. My hands were cold. Not from the air, but with fear. My face was wet. Not from the rain, but from tears. And my tears were not from the wind.

8

I Love You and Party

He was in the Dominican Santa Cruz Hospital. The Catholic Hospital on Soquel. The one right next to Oakwood Cemetery. He didn't even have health insurance. He was against it on principle, always ranting on about the fact that we were the only country in the First World, aside from South Africa, that didn't have proper socialized medicine. It was the bureaucracy. The forms. He'd rather die than fill out a form. I had been born at home in a bathtub in about three inches of warm water. It was an unassisted birth. My dad had cut the umbilical cord.

He was in a coma. An SUV had hit his motorcycle at an intersection. The driver had been talking on his cell phone and had run a red light. Witnesses said the man broke down when he realized what he'd done. Now he was talking to his insurance company and lawyers. We're lucky he stopped, everybody was saying.

My father looked well, when I first saw him. His face was

still tan from living in Karachi. He looked restful, his bronzed
face offset by the cold white of the pillowcase. I had been
expecting black eyes, missing teeth, a fat lip, a broken nose,
lacerations, a shaved head. His injuries were internal, the doc-
tors told me. Damage to his brain and liver. He was all
hooked up to tubes and monitors. He had his own room, the
television left wastefully on, flashing away in the corner with
the sound down.

There was a limit on how long I could stay in there. The
whole room was like some kind of morbid art installation, and
the nurses kept guiding me gently toward the guest lounge.

Dan stayed with me for the first twenty-four hours. He
knew all about me now. He'd tracked me down through my
former Geary Street landlord. They had The Cherry Tree
listed as my place of work. Dan had gone to the club looking
for me. He'd talked to Mac, who'd checked his files for my
emergency contact. When Dad had gone to Pakistan, I'd
changed my "next of kin" to Mary. Mary's contacts were her
parents, who still lived in Sacramento and had referred Dan
back to Mary's new address in San Francisco. It was Mary
who had given him directions to Empire Grade.

I couldn't look at Dan while he relayed the details of his
search. I looked down at *Sunset, Home and Garden,* and *People*
magazines. Julia Roberts smiled back up at me. "Pretty
Happy Woman" it said in big pink letters.

"What the hell did you think you were doing?" Dan asked finally.

"I just wanted some time away."

"Not that commune. I mean that smutty club."

"Shut up," I screamed. "I liked the smutty club. I'd still be there if it wasn't for you."

We slept and paced and woke and talked. My mouth tasted horrid, all furry and dry like somebody had stuffed me with crumbs of blue cheese while I'd been asleep. I'd left my toothbrush at Stephen's. Dan offered to take me home for a few hours, but I refused to leave. The last thing I wanted was to be in my dad's house alone with Dan. So he went alone. I hardly blamed him. He looked like a homeless person, all rough and unshaven, slurring his words. I suppose he always looked a bit like that, but his laid-back hippy vibe had quite disappeared. He was burdened and sad now, angry and tired. And although I didn't go with him, he walked away so heavily it was as though he had the weight of my stubborn, immobile body slung across his shoulders.

I woke up to the sound of a child crying, my face pressed into green-gray, institutional upholstery. A nurse handed me a cup of coffee. There had been no change. I used the bathroom, splashed water on my face, and took a walk around the parking lot. It was early, quiet, the sun only just now easing itself in happy, yellow oblivion over the horizon.

When I returned to the waiting lounge, the morning papers had come. The *San Francisco Chronicle* led with some story about a nurses' strike. But The *Santa Cruz Sentinel* had quite a different headline. I tugged it violently from the overstuffed news rack. As soon as I saw it, depleted as I was, my body channeled a shock so forceful it was as if the wires holding the papers in place carried an electrical charge.

"Missing Girl Found."

I stared at the pages, looking for my name, my picture. But instead the article carried a photo of a teenager, the girl with the long dark hair and thick brows who had been missing for months. She was sixteen years old and had disappeared from her parents' home in Walnut Creek. Her father was a wealthy business entrepreneur. I'd already seen him on TV. Her real name was Elizabeth Jane Skyler. It was Cindy.

Below the headline, all the way down the page and continued on page six, came the whole story. "Missing Teen Discovered in Mountain Eco Cult."

Elizabeth Jane Skyler, the East Bay teen who went
missing from her parents' East Bay home over a year
ago, has finally been reunited with her parents, Len
and Judy Skyler of Castle Rock Road in Walnut Creek.
Skyler was discovered in hiding in a secluded commune

in the Santa Cruz mountains after a surprise raid on the home by the FBI early Thursday morning. The house on Empire Grade, owned by former businessman Stephen Flanders, had been the subject of an undercover federal probe to locate suspected members of an "eco-terrorist" organization, the self-described Earth Liberation Front. Though unable to give details of the operation, FBI spokesperson Alan Fish indicated that Flanders had been linked with a number of acts of so-called "eco terrorism," and several e-mails containing calls for violent action had eventually been traced to his home. It is reported that a federal agent infiltrated the commune, but it was several months between his arrival and the raid.

"We were unable to make a move without sufficient evidence," Fish said. "The ELF is not a particularly large or structured body. Members generally communicate via anonymous e-mail messages, purged of their identifying data. It's the type of underground, grassroots network that anybody can be a part of by self-appointment. These are people who inflict economic damage on any organization engaged in acts of corporate greed or profiteering at the expense of the environment. Their acts of protest often include arson and bomb threats. We really have no idea how many members exist. It could be hundreds, although we suspect its core to be more like fifteen or twenty individuals."

It is thought that Elizabeth Skyler remained unharmed and well cared for while in hiding, and she has described the day-to-day existence as the house as "peaceful."

"It was like a second family," she told reporters during a tearful reunion with her parents Friday afternoon. She has also said she was "unaware" of Flanders' illegal activities.

But during its raid on Flanders' mountain home, agents discovered a basement filled with amateur bomb-making materials and a small number of explosives. It is thought that members of the household may have been planning an attack on a new branch of the drugstore franchise Save Rite, which opened in downtown Santa Cruz just days ago. Police also seized Flanders' computer, which was located in the small basement office. Flanders was placed under arrest and taken into custody.

Also discovered at the house were activists Edward Solario and Nicole Skelly. Solario was previously arrested in 1996 during an investigation into an arson attack on an SUV sales lot in Reno, NV, that did $500,000 worth of damage. He was later acquitted. Between 1992 and 1995, Skelly served a jail term for damage inflicted to a development of newly constructed ski lodges in Vail, Colorado.

It is thought that two other remaining members of the communal household, Skyler and a forty-seven-year-old Chicago woman identified as Margot Dow, were not directly involved in any criminal acts.

"We are treating the Skyler case as runaway," Fish *told* The Sentinel. *"She had clearly disguised her appearance so as not to be found. Though she rarely left the house, Elizabeth has expressed that Flanders, and other household members were unaware of her identity and she was not held against her will."*

Skyler apparently ran away from home thirteen months ago and took a bus to Santa Cruz. It was there that she hooked up with Flanders, who began talking to her in a local grocery store. Though details are still unclear, officials believe she posed as a twenty-one-year-old graduate and that Flanders offered her a room.

The secluded mountain house did not contain a telephone and there was no mail delivery to the address. Household members apparently grew their own food in a crude garden farm, making visits to nearby Felton, Boulder Creek, and Ben Lomand for reserves.

"We're just delighted and relieved to be safely reunited with our daughter," said Len Skyler, *adding that he was* "unlikely" *to press kidnapping charges. Judy Skyler, however, said that she was* "angry and confused" *at the incompetency of the FBI and their*

handling of the probe into Flanders and would expect
a full inquiry as to why the raid and the arrests were
not made sooner.

They didn't identify John, but I knew it was him. I thought about his stories and his university sweatshirts. I wondered about his demeanor, his biography. I tried to remember every word that had come from his mouth and whether it was all part of his cover. His math degree from UMass. His clothes. The things he said. "I adore this time of day," and "I love you." I wondered about hepatitis B and whether he'd really ever had it. I pictured him clean-cut, clean shaven, talking into his watch in a dark suit and with a Mormon haircut.

I thought about the life stories of all the others, and wondered if it really mattered if they were who they said they were, or said who they really were. In the end it didn't really matter to me what they were. It really only mattered what they were like.

Dad did not improve. He didn't stir, his eyelids didn't flicker. I asked him questions and he didn't squeeze my hand. He just breathed. He breathed more than I did. I sat like a stone, waiting and thinking, reading and sleeping.

And I stared at the TV. Elizabeth was on four times a night for about two days, and pictures of Stephen, and his house wrapped up in orange tape. And then the striking nurses took over. Then a movie about a champion racehorse, a fashion show, a cartoon about dolphins, a game show with flashing squares and contestants pressing buzzers and winning prizes. Women in red swimsuits pulling people out of the water. The weather. The sports. Foul balls and kids with big, pointy Styrofoam fingers and umpires yelling into coaches' faces half an inch away from each other. Wrestlers slamming one another into the ground and roaring silently, pounding exploding arms into the air, running sweaty hands through bleached, brittle hair.

And then, on still another channel, the restful shades of black and white. The scratches of old newsreel. A serious documentary with no commercials. Crowds of screaming girls. Old buildings and policemen with dome-shaped helmets looking embarrassed, holding back the throng. It was London. The sixties. Miniskirts. Over-designed hair and horn-rimmed glasses adding decades to teenage girls, lending gawkiness instead of sophistication. Some were laughing as though watching a circus, some crying as though witnessing a horrible train wreck. It was the Beatles, leaving a theater in a modest black car. And then I saw her. She ducked under a policeman's arm. She was tall and slender and wore knee-high white boots and a beehive hairdo. She caught up with the car as it pulled away, and leaned over smiling, to catch a glimpse of George and Ringo. She knocked on the window and waved, and Ringo Starr waved back. Then she tripped, and put her hand up to her mouth, not believing what she'd done. She looked into the camera. She looked right at me. She looked just like me. And though she was about seven years younger, she still looked older than I was. She would have to be, because she was my mother.

I covered my mouth too, and a second passed while we looked into each other's eyes, before she snapped instantly away, and I was left with color video of a bearded music historian, sitting in front of a piano and a bookcase.

My father's body jiggled gently back and forth as I shook him by the shoulders, over and over again. Hurry up and come back. There's so much you don't know. Guess what just happened. Guess who I just saw.

Of all the things I had to tell him, I just wanted to tell him about that. But he never did come back. I wondered how long I'd been sitting in the room watching the television with him already dead.

I went into town and bought him a shirt. It was Dan's idea. Apparently you were supposed to be buried in a suit, like you were getting married or appearing in court. He didn't seem to have a proper shirt; I checked all the closets and drawers. It was all funny button-down collars, or short sleeves, T-shirts, sweatshirts. The blue wool sweater in the top of his bedroom dresser still had strands of his hair stuck to the sleeves. I buried my face in it. It had his smell. A smell that only existed without him there. I'd never noticed it when he was around.

It was the bathroom soap, and candlewax and wood. I cried into the fabric alone in his room. It had been so long, I couldn't remember the last time. Not like that, with the sobbing and noise and everything. So much wet, all over my face and hair. It wasn't like I was crying, it was like I was leaking. And it went on and on until I was simply exhausted and dry.

We determined he was about the same size as Dan, who said he "thought" he was a collar size 16, and 34 or 35 sleeve. He'd only ever had to buy a dress shirt once before, when he had to appear in court on a drunk-driving charge back in 1976.

I went all the way to Eli Thomas Menswear across from the Winchester Mystery House and picked something out. Simple white cotton, and a black silk tie. The gray haired man at the counter asked me if I wanted it gift wrapped.

"That's OK," I said. "It's just something I had to pick up for my father."

"You've made a fine choice," the man said. "He'll like that."

Dan really stood by me that week. The day before the funeral, I went to Save Rite to buy him a card. It was all I could do to salvage what little respect he might, by virtue of some blockage in the drain, have left for me. The array of greeting card categories was quite vulgar in its scope. Friends, Death of a Pet, Thank You, Over the Hill, Happy Birthday Half Brother, Get Well Nephew, Deepest Sympathy. There was an enormous section of cards under the heading "Cope," with a variety of gratuitous greetings on subjects like divorce, sexually trans-mitted diseases, and loss of limb. Among them, I even found a subsection labeled "Lite Cope," presumably for life's more trivial worries like parking tickets, dead plants, and the IRS.

As I flipped through them all, I heard that voice again, coming over the public address system.

"Manager to the monitor room."

It was the same white-bread voice, same inflection as the last time I was in there, buying the laundry soap. Not just sim-ilar sounding, but exactly the same. And I realized that it was just a sound byte, cut into the music. It was probably edited into all the recorded Muzak from Santa Cruz to Carson City. There was no person on the paging system looking out for shoplifters. No manager was about to drop everything and rush to some Pentagon-like monitor center in the back of the store to pass judgment on the guilt or innocence of a drugstore shopper. It was all just a deterrent. They weren't watching you at all. They just wanted you to *think* they were.

I selected a Monet, blank inside, and sat on my bed with it, back at the empty house. Dan had gone home. He'd offered, rather awkwardly, to stay, but what would we do in the house of my dead parents, without a TV?

I clicked the retractable ballpoint in and out, wondering what to say.

"Dear Dan." Dear Dan what? "Dear Dan . . ."

Sorry.

Thank you.

I hope one day we can talk . . .

Although I feel we can never really talk . . .

You've always been like a second father to me . . .

Although nothing can replace my father . . .

Please be there for me.

I will always be there for you.

I need to be alone.

Terrible. I might as well have bought one with the schmaltz preprinted. In the end I wrote, "Dan, Thanks for your help and support during this sad and difficult time" and then never gave it to him.

I moved back up to San Francisco and applied to graduate schools to study literature for the spring. Rents had almost doubled in the time I'd been gone, but I invested the money I obtained when I sold the house in Santa Cruz and tried to live off the interest for a while. I managed to get a studio in Noe Valley for $950. Daylight robbery. It was a nice enough neighborhood, but a bit on the safe side.

Dan left me alone after that. He called every now and then, just to check in. But he met a woman down in Santa Cruz and they moved in together. She was a massage therapist. The real kind, the kind that went to school and worked in a spa and bodywork center. A few months after my father died, Dan called to tell me about her, and a couple of weeks after that she was pregnant and they were thinking of getting married. He sounded really excited.

I talked to him more that night than I ever had in my life. I lay back on my bed and stared at the ceiling, listening to him stream on happily about his plans. He sounded like a newborn Christian, or somebody in AA, apologizing in every sentence for his existence to date.

"You're not that bad," I said. "If you were an old yogurt in my fridge, I'd still peel your lid off and sniff you."

"And what then?"

"I'd stir you up a little, put a little of you on the tip of my tongue, and see how you tasted."

"You little minx," he said. "Don't you ever learn?"

"Sorry," I giggled. "Old habits die hard."

Eventually, there was a small news story on my missing persons case. Since I wasn't as young or as wealthy as Elizabeth/Cindy, I never made the headlines. One hundred thirty thousand people were reported missing in California in 1997 alone. If we were all on the news, there'd be no time for basketball, heat waves, and giraffes being born at the zoo. But I did get an inch in the

Chronicle and a couple of columns in the *Santa Cruz Sentinel.* It caught the eye of the producers of the David Slaughter talk show, and they invited me on to talk about the Eco Cult bust.

I didn't get much airtime. I was sandwiched between a self-help author and a scientist explaining his theory that AIDS had originated with the polio vaccine. I sure had fun, though. Slaughter was still a great big asshole, so I really came out of my shell. I was always more comfortable around assholes. Ultimately, it was honesty and kindness that made me nervous.

"How many members belonged to this Eco Cult?"

"It wasn't a cult.

"Were you brainwashed?"

"Not by them."

"So what did you do up there, in the mountains with these militant hippies?"

"Mostly nap, cook, play, and do the chores."

"Sounds more like summer camp. Were you ever incited to act violently against any individual or corporation?"

"No. They never got around to recruiting me. There were a few friends and hangers-on who were never really hip to what the rest of the group were up to."

"So it was a house share first, a terrorist organization second."

"You could say that."

"One of the tabloids reported that the young girl, the sixteen-year-old, Elizabeth Skyler, was sexually involved with the cult leader, Stephen Flanders. Is there any truth to that?"

"He wasn't a cult leader."

He gave me a sharp stare across the broadcasting booth and adjusted his headphones.

"And if you had been asked to join them in the planned arson attack, or other acts of eco-terrorism, would you have participated?"

"Of course not."

"Why not."

"Because I'd be afraid that innocent people would get hurt."

He laughed. "So you still believe in the concept of innocent people?"

"Yes. Don't you?"

"I do now," he said.

One afternoon, I ran into Mary on Twenty-fourth Street. It was one of those balmy September days, and she was wearing a colorful dress and white sandals. Holding her hand, with the tip of his nose buried in a pink ice cream, was a small boy.

"How are you?" we both asked.

"Good. Great," we both replied.

"So . . . ?" she said.

"Yeah, back in the big city," I said.

The boy tugged at Mary's skirt and silently tried to hand me his collapsing cone.

"And what's your name?" I asked, bending toward him slightly.

The boy just stared at me, smiled again, and wiped his face on Mary's thigh.

"Shy," I said.

"Actually, he can't hear you," Mary said. "He's deaf."

"I see," I said. "So—who's his dad?"

"Robert Grapaldi. Lawyer. Lives in Pacific Heights."

"You're with a lawyer?"

"No. But his mother is," she continued. "Sarah Grapaldi. A painter."

"Buildings or pictures?"

"Buildings," Mary went on. "Thanks for asking. Most people assume bowls of fruit. And this is Robert Jr., their son. Not mine. Deaf but talks. I'm learning sign language and working in education for the hearing impaired."

"That's cool!" I said, like an adolescent cheerleader. I really meant it, though.

"Well, I've only just started. I know two signs. This one . . ." She crossed her forearms over her heart. "And this one . . ." Thumbs and little fingers jangling by her ears.

"And what does that mean?"

"'I love you' and 'Party.'"

"What more does a girl need?"

I walked past The Cherry Tree one day, on the way to City Lights books. They'd gotten rid of the eighties headshots out front and replaced them with a flashing neon silhouette of woman's body. It flickered on and off like a crude cartoon. A girl stood outside smoking. She looked about twelve. She had white, smooth skin and black hair. Her skinny legs seemed contracted and tense in the afternoon chill, and she jiggled up and down to keep warm. I looked past her into the entrance. There were a couple of new doormen, and they'd replaced the carpet. It was plum now, instead of red.

The girl at the door noticed me gazing inside. She stepped on her spent cigarette, grinding it aggressively into the sidewalk like some kind of hotshot dominatrix.

"Don't be shy," she said. "Women are welcome. Everybody's welcome."

"Does Keith Macintosh still run this place?" I asked.

The girl rolled her eyes. "When he feels like it," she said. "How do you know Big Mac?"

"I used to work here," I said.

"Oh yeah? Why'd you leave?"

"Shoes didn't fit. I kept tripping over," I said. "How do you find it?"

"I answered an ad in the paper. They hire anybody who shows up."

"Thanks," I said. "Now I don't feel special anymore. Anyway, that's not what I said. I meant how do you like it?"

"Best job I ever had," replied the girl.

"What other jobs have you had?" I asked.

She said, "I've worked at a law office, I worked for the ACLU, I was a waitress, an administrative assistant, and a theater usher."

"And why do you like this one so much?" I asked. "It was a little slippery for me."

She said, "That's your problem. This is a good job. We're thinking of unionizing. One of the clubs up the street did it. They're part of the Service Employees Local 790. They negotiated for five whole months. Automatic hourly increases, sick days, guaranteed shifts. The works. Of course, this job's a little easier for me than it is for some people. Some of the customers are a little creepy. But I'm not really into guys like that."

I wondered whether she meant "not guys like *that*" or "*Not into them* like that," but she went back inside before I had a chance to ask.

And then there was John. John came back. He showed up on my doorstep, quite dramatically without calling, holding a large pillowcase. His hair was longer now than before, and he had grown a full beard. Not the cop cut, clean shave, and tie I would have expected. He wore jeans and an old leather jacket and he was suntanned.

"Hi Juliet. I brought your stuff," he said from the doorstep, casual as the mailman. He'd kept it all intact inside the pillowcase I'd packed on the night I left Empire Grade.

"I didn't go through it or anything," he said.

We took a walk. I wasn't quite ready to ask him in.

It was awkward and platonic at first. Hard to believe we'd actually seen each other naked. So strange how that chasm between people opens and closes, with the passing of a few weeks or months. One minute you're buried in the folds of each other's flesh, the next you're two feet apart on a sidewalk, looking in divergent directions at shops and houses and bus stop billboards. He took in the details of the latest cellular phone technology, while I observed that garden furniture was half off.

He accidentally brushed against me with his swinging arm and we pretended not to notice. I sneezed and giggled, and he said "bless you," which helped break the ice a little.

We wandered up to the park and walked up toward the kids' play area. I felt jaded and responsible all at once. The story of my life. I wondered what it was about children that always made me so reflective. I didn't think much about ever actually having any of my own. Childhood was something that passed me by, and then it was gone, but like the last noisy slurps of a hot fudge sundae, I couldn't quite let it go.

"How did you find me?"

He gave me a patronizing raise of the eyebrow.

"Oh yeah," I said. "I forgot. You're an FBI agent. Stupid."

"Was. Anyway, you're in the phone book."

"True. Why the hell didn't you call first?"

"Because then you could have said 'No.'"

I said, "What do you mean . . . 'was'?"

"Huh?"

"'Was' an FBI agent?"

"Quit over that stupid Empire Grade fiasco. I took way too long to wrap it up. Missed the Skyler girl entirely. I was actually just a rookie. Made quite a vacation out of it, really. I sort of liked it up there. Didn't you?"

"I liked what I thought it was."

"Didn't know you were a Red Sox fan," he said.

I took off my baseball cap. "I'm not," I said. "It's part of my Baseball Teams I Don't Follow hats collection. I've got this one and a Mets cap."

"Two? Not much of a collection."

We stopped on a bench and I leaned forward, ranting at my shoes.

"Stephen Flanders is in jail because of you! Why didn't you tell me who you were working for? I can't believe you were a federal agent. That's disgusting!"

"Time out, Pussy Longstocking. What's on your resume?"

"Fuck off."

He stood up and started to walk away. I pulled him back.

"Is your name even John?"

"Sure. Aliases are for cowards."

That went a long way with me.

"Good for you," I said. "I never used one even when I did porn."

"That's not too bright."

"Why? I don't want to run for office, do I? I don't want to work for the FBI. Anyway, I don't regret it. It was my choice, and the money was awesome."

"Would you do it again?"

"As long as nobody got hurt. So that sort of rules out bondage, I guess."

"Good God," said John, shaking his head. "I don't know about you. You're as tough as leather, aren't you? Meeting you was like finding somebody's lost wallet. You want to rifle through the contents, see what they're worth, where they live, whether they drive, what video store they rent from, whether they use the library, whose picture they're carrying. Then you're suddenly responsible for doing the right thing, going out of your way to return it safely to wherever it belongs."

What a snoop, I thought. He should have stuck with the Feds, after all.

"John," I asked, "when you asked me what I thought about that planned arson on the Nike shop in Minnesota . . . were you just testing me?"

He said, "Not—no."

I looked over to the playground. A young man about my age was playing with his daughter on the swings, pushing her higher and higher, the girl squealing with fear and delight each time she was thrust toward the sky.

We sat quietly for a moment, watching pigeons peck happily away at a puddle of dog vomit.

"My dad died," I said.

It really sliced into him. I could see it in his face, like he'd swallowed something huge and indigestible like human flesh or pieces of glass. He didn't speak or move for about thirty seconds. Then he turned to me with a dark, grown-up stare, and started to say something.

"Juliet. That's—that's," he stammered.

"That's very sad," I said, composed, at first. "It was an accident. A road accident. He lived for a few days, then died in the hospital. I never even got to talk to him. He was in a coma. You know how people are supposed to blink and hold your hand? Well, he didn't. He was like a crash test dummy. Limp and silent.

"When I was going through his stuff, back at the house, books and clothes and pictures and records and coffee mugs, and putting it in boxes, I kept stopping on things and thinking I should go out in the garden and ask him first whether he wanted to keep them or not. I was going to have a yard sale, but how could I make money off the back of that? I gave most of it to the Salvation Army. I think he would have liked that.

"I miss my mother more now. Not my mother, herself. Just having one. I never missed having one before, but just one parent would be nice. Some days I feel like I've been dumped off on the first day of school and nobody's ever going to come and pick me up. You're supposed to grow up when you're parents die, but I want to be tucked in and read to. I want tomato soup and Christmas presents."

"I'll get you soup and presents," said John.

"I didn't mean that. I can get my own," I said, horrified at my own pitiful whining.

He even offered me a handkerchief. It was embroidered with the words "Brigham Young."

"Mormons?" I said, throwing it back to him. "Ugh. I'll use my sleeve."

I don't know what horrified me more. My self-pity, and how much I waded around in it, or that nobody else seemed to mind or notice. I always expected someone either to pull me out and throw me under a cold shower, or push my head down and keep it there.

And then John looked up at the sky with his hands behind his head and did just that.

"My mother died three weeks ago. We lost my father about twenty years ago, but she'd just remarried. They lived in Vermont. New house and everything. My stepdad's still there. I haven't even told him I lost my job. He's not doing too well. I'll have to visit him again soon. You can come with me, if you like. I guess he's pretty lonely."

The girl on the swing was still going, leaning backward now, her hair brushing against the ground at the bottom of the swing's arc, then swooping upward toward the trees and back again.

"The whole world's upside down!" she said.

"Upside down, is it?" said her father. "Is it the world, or is it you?"

And gradually the swing slowed. John and I sat and watched together from our bench as its trajectory became twisted, its graceful swaying corrupted by the little girl wriggling impatiently to get off. Finally, she slowed down enough to put her feet down and jump to the ground. The man reached out to catch her, but she ducked through his arms and ran off toward the street.

I did go to Vermont with John. We stayed in Burlington, voted number three safest and most livable city in the country. I looked around for the famous coat factory, but it turned out to be in Burlington, New Jersey. We toured the ice cream factory instead, and returned to San Francisco once John's stepfather's spirits were more intact, if not sunny, and the weather had fallen apart.

We grew closer, then apart again, then into friends. With his inheritance John bought a place a few blocks from mine, and we went from friends to close again.

I bought a motorcycle, John bought a car, and we went on trips, long weekends like repeated honeymoons without the hassle of a wedding. Bodega Bay, home of Hitchcock's demented birds; Lake Tahoe, where we braved a swim and risked death from hypothermia and the controversial fuel emissions recently found in the water; Yosemite National Park where I left the camera on a picnic table next to the visitors' center. We were forty miles out of there before I realized.

"Forget it," I said. "I might have forgotten the camera, but I'll remember the experience."

"Oh, so will I," John said. "I bought postcards. But that was a four-hundred-dollar camera."

And he turned the car around and we went back for it. It was still there on the table among some scraps of hot dog bun.

Sometimes, when I was afraid of the future, I would look at those ads for adult models and dancers and escorts, promising thousands of dollars a week for part-time work. I felt like a retired criminal, intermittently summoned from the poolside as my loved ones drank piña coladas and barbecued ribs in the background, still somehow liable to be lured back for "one last job." And this is the last one, I promise.

John caught me once, fingering down the "Adult Help Wanted" ads, one free morning at the kitchen table, with a cup of coffee and momentarily idle hands.

I quickly flipped the page. But it was too late. He'd seen it.

"You know how that makes me feel?" he said. "It makes me sick."

And for a confusing moment, I didn't know what disturbed

me more. That I had it in me to make him sick, or that he was telling me I did.

I suddenly had this image of myself as the topic du jour on a lurid daytime talk show, with some fat, angry woman yelling at me:

"Yeah, I just wanna say something to you on the right, the blond bitch. Yeah, this guy who really cares about you, he's asking you not to do some fucked-up pussy-flashing shit, but you're too vain and greedy to listen. You don't care about anyone but yourself. I don't care how much you could be pulling in. You better think about some other people or you're going down, girlfriend."

And then this skinny chick on the other side, with big lip-stick and funky hair, going:

"I think, what's-her-name, the blonde, she respects herself just fine. Women are always doing what we're told. She's sicka THAT shit. She was making good money for some-thing she's good at. If people can't deal with it, that's their problem. Why's it always men, tryna tell us what to do, and shit? Tryna control us and give us shit for something they like looking at as long as it's some other bitch doing the work. You go, girl!"

They yelled at each other for a while in my head, until I was so tired of listening to this mouthy internal debate, I took it as a sign that I didn't have it in me at all any more. The impulse hadn't fully spent itself, but something had changed.

It was like I was still trying to sell my soul to the devil, but the devil just wasn't having any of it.

"Well, it's a bit patched up, isn't it? I mean, I've seen worse souls, of course, but I really prefer them mint-in-box, brand-new-to-excellent condition. It's not in bad shape, yours, but it's *used,* isn't it? It's a repair job, eh?"

"But I've had all the right experience. I'm a real work-horse. How about a second chance?"

"Sorry, love. You just don't fit my current needs."

"But I—"

"Look, thanks for the offer, but I really can't use you. I'm a little oversubscribed right now."

For the first time, I thought about how my mother would have felt, had she known. How my father would have reacted had he found out. Everything was different without him there to catch me at it or set me straight. Without him around to make his case, I respected his sensibilities all the more. It was all as though I'd been trusted with the keys to a fine, new home, and I was damned if I was going to disappoint, to blow it all and have a party and get sick on the carpet now. It just wasn't going to happen.

And when I brought it up, one last time, to John, one final "but the money was good" comment over a contemplative risotto dinner, he pushed his chair away from the table, and said I didn't understand love, and punched the picture frame, so that the glass broke and cut his hand, and blood dripped all over the rug.

It was a little macho for me. But ultimately this was such an uncharacteristically raw and straightforward reaction it got through to me more than anything he had ever said.

I guess it wasn't really like selling my soul, or a life of high crime. It was probably more like gambling. You might feel rich for a while, but in the end you have to take into consideration what you could lose.

I sleep better now. But every now and then I still have dreams that don't belong in my room. Visions of stale skin pressing against my face so that I can't breathe. Scenes of John looking at naked pictures of me on the Internet, and then dressing me from head to toe with computer graphic designer clothes in Photoshop. Glimpses of the Santa Cruz Mountains from down on the beach where I am kite flying, where I can see a hazy, smoky glow, and sooty black clouds spreading across the sky above the trees in the hills where Stephen's house used to be. And when I open my eyes, there is always a second or two before it is all gone, before my muddled recollections give way to the white shades on the windows and the sounds of the street outside, a brief moment in which these burlesque apparitions linger in the room, somewhere between the carpet and the ceiling.

About the Author

Laura Denham was born in London in 1966 and grew up in Jamaica, Jordan, and the Isle of Wight in England. Her writing has appeared in Salon.com, *The San Francisco Bay Guardian, Fiction, The South Dakota Review, The Beloit Fiction Journal, 580 Split, Foliage Short Story Quarterly, Phoebe, The Evansville Review,* and other journals. She lives in San Francisco.